GW00726782

Bone

Dry

A Salt Mine Novel

Joseph Browning   Suzi Yee

Text Copyright © 2020 by Joseph Browning and Suzi Yee

Published by Expeditious Retreat Press
Cover by J Caleb Design
Edited by Elizabeth VanZwoll

For information regarding Joseph Browning and Suzi Yee's novels and to subscribe to their mailing list, see their website at https://www.joseph-browning.com

To follow them on Twitter: https://twitter.com/Joseph_Browning

To follow Joseph on Facebook: https://www.facebook.com/joseph.browning.52

To follow Suzi on Facebook: https://www.facebook.com/SuziYeeAuthor/

To follow them on MeWe: https://mewe.com/i/josephbrowning

By Joseph Browning and Suzi Yee

THE SALT MINE NOVELS

Money Hungry	Hen Pecked	Dark Matter
Feeding Frenzy	Brain Drain	Silent Night
Ground Rules	Bone Dry	Better Half
Mirror Mirror	Vicious Circle	Soul Mates
Bottom Line	High Horse	Swan Song
Whip Smart	Fair Game	Deep Sleep
Rest Assured	Double Dutch	

Chapter One

Lafayette, Louisiana, USA
24th of January, 3:45 p.m. (GMT-6)

Zoe Miller paused, her hand hovering just over the intercom button as she intently watched the antique clock on the wall. It didn't matter that it was already 3:45 on her phone; the office clock was the official time as far as the boss was concerned. Every so often, she would climb on a chair and reset it when the lag became too unbearable, but there was never a question of replacing it with one of those radio-controlled clocks. Accurate time was hardly worth sacrificing all that history and charm.

Her grandmother always said a watched pot never boils, but she couldn't help herself. All afternoon, her eyes kept wandering back to the bold black Roman numerals against the white enamel that had yellowed over time. Tomorrow was the Lunar New Year, which meant tonight would be filled with fireworks and dragon dances, if one knew where to look for such things in Louisiana.

Last year's celebration had opened her up to a whole new world of Chinese food beyond fried rice and sweet and sour pork. Poultry and fish with the heads still on, mounds of noodles made from different kinds of flour, steamed cakes, fried dumplings both sweet and savory, and those little sweet toffees wrapped in rice paper that melted on her tongue… Just the thought made her salivate and she'd eaten a light lunch to make sure she brought her appetite to the festivities.

Zoe rolled her eyes as the minute hand tortuously twitched, not quite mustering the momentum to inch toward the nine on the dial. Suddenly, her phone buzzed in her other hand with an update: a picture of the latest batch of golden sesame balls fresh from the fryer. She could almost taste the sweetened red bean paste encased in the chewy, crusty exterior.

Her friend, who had taken the day off work to cook up a storm with her family, had been sending pictures all day. Zoe liked the photo and tapped out a quick one-handed reply in emojis that essentially translated to: *you're killing me, Smalls!*

Message sent, she swept her large brown eyes back to the chipped enamel face and glared hard, as if sheer will were enough to hasten the passage of time. When the minute hand finally lurched forward, she depressed the button, worn smooth by years of wear and use. A crackle came over the speakers dotted throughout the premises.

She leaned into the microphone and employed her customer service voice. "Ladies and Gentlemen, the time is 3:45. We will be closing in fifteen minutes. Please wrap up your visit in a timely fashion. Thank you for visiting the Acadian Village and come on back another day. *Au revoir!*" She simultaneously released the button and her cheerful facade and started closing up the office.

She did one last scan of the paperwork before filing it behind last week's. As a nonprofit, they had to keep meticulous records of everything to retain their status, and her knack for numbers and navigating bureaucracy had been quickly recognized and put to good use. She collected the cash from the drop box and collated it for deposit. As a necessity of the times, they accepted credit cards but they preferred cash. Accepting hard currency didn't cost merchant fees, and every penny added up.

Zoe systematically locked all the cupboards and filing cabinets, giving them a slight jiggle for confirmation. She grabbed the walkie-talkie from the charging station to check in with the event coordinator before making the rounds. "Eva, it's Zoe. How's everything going? Over."

"Like herding cats with a shoddy broom. Over," a voice came over the line with a drawl so thick it managed to find two syllables in *broom*.

Zoe curtly laughed before replying. "Listen, I'm about to do the closing pass. Am I supposed to keep any of the buildings open for tonight? Over."

"No, you can close everything else up except for the chapel. Just make sure there are no malingering guests. The mother of the bride is chomping at the bit to get it ready for the ceremony. I have never seen so much tulle," she confessed before addressing someone else in the room, "Hey, you can't put that there. It's blocking a fire exit." Zoe heard Eva's tinny rebuke scratch through the small speaker; even the walkie-talkies were old. "You wanna trade jobs, just for tonight? Over." The tone was light but there was earnestness behind the veneer of humor.

"Not for all the tea in China. You do people, I do numbers. Never shall the twain meet. Over," Zoe stated emphatically as she grabbed her windbreaker and the hefty ring of keys from the closet.

"All right, but don't blame me if bridezilla or her mother ends up in the canal. Over," Eva said sweetly under her breath.

"Why not both? The canal's big enough. Over," Zoe offered drily.

Eva feigned innocence. "You're gonna get me in trouble. Don't you have work to do? Over."

"I'm leaving the office now. Holler if you need me to stop you from chucking anyone off a bridge. Over and out." Zoe signed off and clipped the walkie-talkie to her belt. She stepped out into the dying light of late afternoon and was immediately transported back two hundred years. A gust of wind rustled the leaves of the majestic canopies surrounding the stalwart cypress homes. They had survived this long and on different soil; a little wind wasn't going to knock them over now.

The Acadian Village was a recreation of a typical 1800s Cajun village, complete with its own manufactured bayou crossed with bridges. It was owned and operated by the

Lafayette Association for Retarded Citizens, which now went by the acronym LARC to avoid the problematic language of the past. In the 1970s, the association transformed ten acres of its land into what it hoped would become a tourism destination to supplement the ever-dwindling government funding. Little did LARC know how popular it would become to locals and tourists alike.

All the structures in the village proper were of historic value, seven of which were authentic homes taken from all over Louisiana— donations from the families whose ancestors once lived under those high-peaked roofs. They were painstakingly moved to Lafayette piece-by-piece and sympathetically restored, down to the deer hair plaster and whitewashed brick.

Inside, many of the homes were converted to showcase different aspects of 1800s life. What wasn't original were faithful reproductions built with period materials, true to the resourceful spirit of the Cajuns. The blacksmith's workshop was constructed out of aged, weather-beaten cypress boards, the preferred wood used by the Cajuns due to its resistance to rot and insects in the warm, wet environment they made their homes. And then, there was La Chapelle de Nouvel Espoir— New Hope Chapel for those that didn't speak French. It was a replica of an 1850 Acadian chapel, built with a cypress ceiling and a sealed and waxed floor of Louisiana long leaf pine that was two hundred years old.

When Zoe first started working here, she hadn't intended to

stay long. It was just something to pay the bills until she found something better. However, the longer she remained, the less appealing moving on became. The pay wasn't great, but it was enough and she was doing something meaningful. She never had been all that interested in Cajun culture, but if it helped fund those with intellectual and developmental disabilities live as independently as possible with dignity and self-worth, then *laissez les bons temps rouler*.

Zoe locked the door to the office, inconspicuously located within the donated 1890 home of Lafayette's first resident dentist, and zipped up her jacket. It was cool, but hardly cold; it was what passed for winter in these parts.

Zoe systematically made a circuit along the winding brick-laid paths and wooden bridges, gently encouraging any stragglers she encountered toward the exit. Along the way, she entered each building to check the displays, turn off any lights, and lock the doors on her way out.

Zoe veered toward the bridge leading to the chapel, her last stop of the night. Her steps resonated on the wooden planks and off the still water below. It was a straight shot to the front door of the chapel, making it one long procession into the house of worship. The limbs of a willow languidly draped and skirted the ground on the other side, lending the approach some natural grace.

The New Hope Chapel bore all the marks of Acadian construction. A simple cross topped the bell tower and the narrow front vestibule stood proud against the wings, all covered by a sharply angled cypress-shingled roof. The structure was whitewashed brick, and inside, the large beams and wooden ceiling were exposed. There were ten short rows of hand-carved wooden pews on either side of the center aisle, all but one replicas, fashioned after the twentieth pew—a 150-year-old original. The chapel's reconstruction was a love letter to Cajun craftsmanship; even the pews' joints were pegged with wooden nails. However, there were a few concessions that had to be made for modern times, notably electricity and air conditioning.

By modern standards, it was quite modest in size, holding less than 100 people by the village's recommendation, but it was quite impressive for the time and would have been the center of village life in the 1800s. It was perfect for small weddings, especially daytime ceremonies in summer when the light streamed in through the arched stain glass windows and the air conditioning spared everyone the indignity of melting in the heat.

Historically, Acadians were Catholic with a capital C, and wherever they landed, they kept their faith, music, food, and their French language, even if it had evolved into its own dialect during their time in Louisiana. Although the chapel was a non-denominational space that had not been consecrated by the Catholic Church, there was plenty of iconography to harken back to Acadian religious roots: a hand-carved Stations of the Cross, the plaster of paris main altar—the type used before

Vatican Council II —and a side altar with the Last Supper scene.

Zoe entered the chapel and unzipped her jacket once the door had closed behind her and cut out the wind. She walked up the center aisle, as so many brides had done before and one would do later tonight, but her purpose was altogether different. She was taking stock of the chapel's condition before giving the wedding party access. The renters would be liable for any damage sustained during their event, including set up and tear down.

She was looking over the main altar behind its protective wooden frame when a chill ran down her spine and goose bumps erupted along her skin. She reflexively rubbed her hands over her arms to warm them.

"*Où est Pauline?*" a baritone voice echoed in the high ceiling, causing Zoe to nearly jumped out of her skin. She hadn't heard the door open, but clearly, she wasn't alone.

She turned around and spotted a figure standing in the front vestibule, dressed in a vintage suit, top hat, and dress shoes polished to a high shine. Zoe searched her memory. Was that the bride's name? Or maybe her mother or one of the bridesmaids? The surname was the only one listed on the event schedule, so she covered all bases as she answered back in French.

"The girls are getting ready in the bridal suite while the mother of the bride is overseeing the reception site in the Stutes

Building. Down the path. If you come to the pavilion, you've gone too far."

"*Merci beaucoup*," he replied, touching the brim of his hat before disappearing.

Someone is dressed to impress, she commented to herself as she resumed her inspection—that getup certainly wasn't something purchased off the rack at a big box store, but the smart money was that someone picked it out for him and told him to wear it.

Zoe pulled the walkie-talkie off her belt and opened a channel. "I think I found your groom. I sent him your way. Over."

"Roger," Eva answered in the affirmative. "Can I send the mother of the bride to the chapel yet? Over." *And get her out of my hair was implied.*

"Give me five more minutes and it's all yours. Over and out," Zoe promised. She scanned her checklist one more time. She kept getting the niggling notion that something wasn't right, but she couldn't put her finger on it. She had checked everything and nothing was amiss. She came to the conclusion that the uneasiness in her stomach was hunger and grabbed the walkie-talkie. "Eva, it's Zoe. The chapel's all clear. Over."

She waited for a reply but it was mostly static with snippets of words. "Old piece of junk," she muttered as she slapped it a few times against her thigh before pressing the button again. "I didn't catch that. Can you repeat? Over."

As soon as she released the button, the walkie-talkie crackled and filled with music. Good old Cajun music, complete with foot stomping to keep time in the background. Then the screams started, cutting through the soulful melody.

"Eva, are you all right?" Zoe spoke louder into the walkie-talkie. When there was no answer, her stomach bottomed out and she took off out the chapel's front door. She didn't have a plan, but she hurried even more once she caught the dulcet bow strokes of a fiddle in three-quarter time.

She was nearly at the Stutes Building when the fiddle suddenly stopped and a wail came from within. "*Oh pa janvier, donne moi Pauline!*" A wave of sadness descended upon her and made her steps falter.

As the final notes dissipated, she shrugged off her melancholy and found her footing. As she reached the entrance, however, good sense finally came to her—what if someone dangerous was inside? Her heart was pounding, and she could see her rapid breath in front of her face. She pulled out her phone and tapped 911 on her number pad, with her thumb hovering over "send."

She threw open the door and found the room wrecked. The tables were knocked over and chairs on their sides. A few of the fixtures were shattered, casting uneven light at odd angles on the floor. Balls of tulle rolled across the floor like frosted pink tumbleweed across the marbles that once filled the toppled centerpieces. Not even the three-tiered wedding cake had been spared, splattered against the wall like raspberry and buttercream plaster.

Unwilling to step inside, she shouted from the threshold, "Eva, are you in there? Is everyone okay?" The quiet was deafening.

She quickly checked the bridal suite and found it in a similar state. Everything had been tossed about, and there was makeup, bobby pins, and flower petals from the battered bouquets strewn across the room. She called out and again was met with silence. Shaken, she hit "send" on her phone and brought it to her ear.

"911, what's your emergency?"

"This is Zoe Miller at the Acadian Village," she conscientiously identified herself and her location. "There was supposed to be a wedding here this evening and something has happened to the wedding party. The place is trashed."

"Is anyone hurt?" the operated asked over his rapid typing.

"I'm not sure," Zoe answered honestly. "Everyone's just up and disappeared."

Chapter Two

Detroit, Michigan, USA
29th of January, 6:00 a.m. (GMT-5)

The alarm sounded, followed shortly by a groan. It was too early and too cold to get up. Teresa Maria Martinez ventured just enough of her body out from under the covers and groped for her mobile. Once it was safely cocooned with her under the heavy comforter, she switched off the alarm and checked the weather: five degrees below zero and twelve inches of accumulation overnight.

"Oh good, it snowed. Again," she said out loud to her empty room. Martinez pulled on her clothes from last night, still sandwiched together in layers. First, she slid her feet into a pair of thick woolen socks that contained a pair of thin cotton tube socks inside, pulling them as high over her calves as possible. Then, she wriggled into the yoga pants that were nestled into her sweat pants. She owned long johns, but the thought of putting them on seemed unduly difficult this morning. Even a bra sounded hard.

Next, she wove her arms through the long-sleeved t-shirt that was underneath another knit top and a sweatshirt. When all three neck openings came into alignment, she popped her head through. She lingered a few more minutes, not long enough to fall back asleep but until her clothes no longer felt cold. After she had captured as much warmth as possible, she slipped out of bed, whipped her hair into a rough bun, and went downstairs.

She stopped by the kitchen to switch on the coffee maker before proceeding to the mudroom, running her hands over the outerwear she'd hung up yesterday: a puffy parka, thick insulated gloves, and a plaid hunter's hat with earflaps. Intellectually, she knew that snow was frozen water, but it still astounded her just how wet everything got when she messed with the white stuff.

It was hard to tell if they were damp because they were cold to the touch, but they were dry enough for the task at hand—the snow wasn't going to move itself off her driveway. In Oregon, a foot of snow would have closed schools and been a passable excuse for a late start at the FBI. In Michigan, it was just another Wednesday—quit your bellyaching and start shoveling. She suited up and pulled on her snow boots, fortifying herself with the thought that she would have a hot cup of coffee waiting for her when she was done.

At first, she had been determined to enjoy the snow. She'd watched the pristine beauty of freshly fallen powder from the warmth of her Corktown home, often with a mug of hot chocolate or tea in hand. She'd made snow angels and snowmen in the backyard. She'd even tried her hand at ice skating in the brisk open air. And there was the undeniable charm of a white Christmas. But as the weeks turned into months, the novelty wore thin.

January was the coldest and driest month in Michigan, but all the precipitation that did fall came down as snow that accumulated, making it the snowiest month of the year. It was the very peak of the season, and there was definitely a Jack London man-versus-nature vibe as Martinez tucked her messy bun into her hat for a snug fit. The garage was chilly but bearable with the heat pouring out of the open vent. There were puddles of water from the snow that had melted off her black Dodge Hellcat overnight. She braced herself for the frigid air before opening the garage door to the dark sky. She felt a little like Elmer Fudd in the getup, except instead of a hunting rifle, she was armed with a Craftsman.

Never one to be caught unprepared, Martinez had gone shopping for a snow blower just as all the Halloween decorations hit the shelves. She'd figured waiting until the first snowfall would only drive the prices up and reduce availability. After weighing all her options, she begrudgingly admitted that she had reached the age where "treat yo' self" meant springing for the deluxe snow blower and purchased a two-stage machine with all the bells and whistles.

Martinez inserted the key and pushed the start button. She'd had enough run-ins with pull-start lawnmowers to elect for an electric start, especially since below-freezing temperatures only made motors more temperamental. As advertised, the cold engine roared to life.

She switched on the headlights from the central control panel, a practical feature given the whopping four hours of sunlight Detroit received on average this time of year. Using the joystick on the console, she adjusted the angle of the discharge chute before attacking the first swath of driveway.

She guided the blower with ease; the self-propulsion and power steering—engaged by a lever on the right handle—took the muscle work out of it. The snow was heavy and wet, but the corkscrew-like augur cut through the sheet of white, pushing it into the center housing before propelling it out the shaft. A snowy arc cleared the ridge from yesterday's plowing, and fat flurries landed on her as the wind picked up stray snowflakes and flung them back into the air. She made quick work of the driveway and her stretch of the sidewalk, adjusting the pitch and orientation of the chute with each change in direction.

There had been a learning curve. It wasn't the sort of thing a West Coast girl had to know. Sure, it sometimes snowed in Oregon, especially in the mountainous regions, but everything just shut down while Oregonians waited for it to melt. For years, the state didn't even salt the roads. And if it snowed during a visit to her dad in Colorado, he would have it taken care of before she even got out of bed. Little did she know how much effort he'd put in while she was asleep so they could simply pull out of the driveway whenever they wanted.

Having the right hardware was just the beginning, and there was definitely a science to it. First, she got a practical refresher on geometry—how to efficiency cover the area with as few passes as possible, and how to angle the chute to get the snow to land where she wanted it. Then she learned that she had to shoot the snow further out than she thought to make sure there was enough space to clear everything, because there might not be significant compaction or melting before the next snowfall. She eventually figured out how to mound the pile without causing mini avalanches later on. And then there was the blowback—just as one should never piss into the wind, the adage also applied to snow blowing.

Once she had cleared the path, Martinez knocked off as much snow as she could from the blower and the tread of the airless tires—a feature that guaranteed she would never have to check tire pressure or air them up at the gas station. No matter the day or time, there was always a ridiculous line to use the "free air" machine.

With the snow blower parked back in the garage, Martinez grabbed a self-fashioned scooper—a plastic gallon milk jug with the top cut off—and filled it full of course salt. She deposited a layer on the newly cleared concrete and asphalt, liberally hitting the walkways and wheel line on the sloped driveway. Salt was one thing she was never short of working at the Salt Mine—the covert black ops agency that monitored supernatural activity.

Finally, she brushed the snow from her outerwear and clapped her gloved hands together before lowering the garage door and hanging everything in the mudroom once more.

Inside the kitchen, she poured herself a hot cup of coffee, warmed her hands on the mug, and bid good morning to the collection of snow figures in the backyard. It had started with a traditional three-tiered snowman, but after her third one, she'd decided to branch out. It was surprising therapeutic to sculpt snow, not unlike building sand castles. The stuff from last night would be perfect for construction—dry powder may be ideal of skiing, but it didn't have enough moisture for the snow to stick together.

As she toyed with what to make next, an ebony cat entered the kitchen and announced her presence with a declarative meow. Martinez smiled behind her cup. "Hello, kitty." The silky Egyptian Mau came closer, her sleek form obscured under her thick winter coat. The cat rubbed against Martinez's leg, tilting her head ever so slightly. Martinez bent down and scratched the feline's ears. The cat purred in delight. She allowed Martinez to pick her up and pet her, burrowing in the human's warmth.

Just as Martinez had gotten Stigma out of her house, she had acquired a part-time pet, and the serendipity of the timing had not been lost on her. *And Aaron was worried I would be lonely without him…* she mused as she stroked the velvety coat.

Technically, the cat was Wilson's, but she seemed to visit with some regularity and at her leisure. It hadn't taken Martinez long to guess that the cat Wilson had brought to Thanksgiving was Mau, the mummified cat of legend that had been stolen last year. She had been retrieved and returned to Hor-Nebwy, the mummy power that reigned over the Valley of the Magi, but how Mau came to live with Wilson after that was beyond Martinez, and she knew better than to ask or speak of it.

She never knew when Mau might appear in her house and kept the cupboard stocked for her impromptu visits. The fact that the cat entered and left the house without anyone opening the door for her was further proof of Martinez's suspicions—there was no place on earth Mau could not go. Still, she kept up the ruse that Mau was just a normal cat, albeit one that could turn ethereal to play with the little ghost girl that lived in the attic.

"Are you hungry?" Martinez asked the nestled ball of fur in her lap. Mau answered in the affirmative with an unambiguous meow. "Then you're going to have to let me get up."

A pair of piercing jade eyes emerged, upturned in slight indignation. Mau begrudgingly took to her feet and leapt to the floor. It seemed colder than before now that she had gotten warm. She bound for the rug before sitting on her haunches, expectantly waiting for the human to bring her food.

Martinez took the opportunity to reheat her own breakfast—oatmeal with honey, cranberries and slivered almonds—before grabbing a can from the pantry. She always had tuna, but sprung for fancy cat food with gravy when it was on sale. They even sold soup for cats now. She scooped the contents into a shallow dish that had become Mau's bowl, a blue on white porcelain she had picked up at a garage sale on a lark.

The microwave dinged as she set the food on the floor, and Mau was face deep in her food by the time Martinez was back in her seat with hers. They breakfasted together in amicable silence until the sound of heavy metal scraping its way down her street broke the quaint, domestic scene. Martinez was grateful to drive on city-plowed and salted roads, but that didn't stop her from grumbling each time she had to re-clear the small line of drift left in its wake on her driveway. "That's my cue to get ready for work," she said to the cat on her way to the sink with the dishes.

Mau, who was performing her postprandial grooming, looked up and gave a sympathetic meow to the Mountain, the name she had bestowed upon Martinez. Of all the things Mau had learned of Detroit since her arrival, the chill of winter was at the bottom of the list. Not even the tomb had been so cold.

Chapter Three

Detroit, Michigan, USA
29th of January, 10:08 a.m. (GMT-5)

Martinez sat outside Leader's office on the fourth floor of the Salt Mine, drumming her fingers against her thigh. She shifted her weight and checked her watch again. It wasn't like Leader to be late for an appointment. The note in her in basket had said 10:00 a.m., hadn't it? She opened her leather bag to double check.

The blond man in the navy suit sitting behind the desk looked up from the computer, making eye contact with a facial expression that boiled down to *I'm sure it will only be a few more minutes*. To which Martinez replied with a head tilt and neutral smile: *Oh, me? I'm fine, continue with your work*. Which was redundant, considering his fingers never stopped moving across the keyboard the entire time.

Martinez pulled out her phone, occupying her hands with a familiar prop. It gave her the perfect excuse to break eye contact with the square-jawed man sitting at LaSalle's desk. She furtively eyed him in her peripheral vision.

His name was Ethan Helms, and he wasn't normally found

below ground. Up until recently, she only saw him outside the penthouse office of Angelica Zervo, CEO of Discretion Minerals—Leader's official alias topside. By her reckoning, he'd taken over LaSalle's duties a week ago—at least, that was when she noticed Helms had approved her latest expense report.

It was strange seeing Helms out of context, like when you run into your doctor at the grocery store in their gym clothes, but equally odd to see someone else at LaSalle's desk. Helms seemed efficient and capable, and Martinez had no doubt about his trustworthiness: if Leader had vetted him, he was good. But he still wasn't LaSalle.

Physically, they were quite different. Helms was average height and of slim build, in stark opposition to LaSalle's imposing stature. It was almost comical how small Helms looked in LaSalle's office chair. She smirked at the thought of his feet dangling behind the wooden front panel, not quite able to touch the ground in order to work at LaSalle's desk.

Though he lacked the bulk, Martinez was not naive enough to assume Helms had no extra-secretarial skills. Lethality came in many shapes and sizes. Look at Wilson—he was a small guy and could incapacitate or kill a target without batting an eye—and Martinez would hate to be on the receiving end of a blade wielded by Liu. Martinez supposed Helms had to have some esoteric proficiency to pass as Leader's assistant underground. At the very least, he had to know about magic: that is was real, that it bore a cost, and his boss kept watch on it.

And there was his demeanor—a hard, cold precision underneath the polite facade. Not that there was anything soft about LaSalle, but his stalwart resolve wasn't frosty. It had allowed Martinez to slowly build up a rapport with Leader's brick of a secretary-slash-bodyguard, something she had no desire to do with Helms.

There were notable behavioral differences that stemmed from that underlying coldness. For example, LaSalle would have spoken to her about the meeting with Leader, not left a note in her in-basket. He would have offered her something to drink if Leader was running late, which rarely happened on LaSalle's watch. He would have addressed her if he felt establishing contact was warranted, not glance over his keyboard and down his nose at her. Calling Helms impersonal would be the polite description.

While she enumerated the ways in which Helms was not LaSalle, the rapid click-clack of his typing stopped long enough for him to answer the phone. "Discretion Minerals," he said in an officious tone on the headset that he never took off. "This is Ms. Zervo's direct line," he confirmed. "This is her assistant. How can I help you?"

Martinez could see her smile in the reflection on her phone—another clue that this was temporary. Helms was still actively taking care of business above ground. That, coupled with the fact that the tight-lipped blond with the cleft chin hadn't reorganized or changed anything at the desk in LaSalle's absence suggested the posting wasn't permanent. Which made her wonder where LaSalle was, what he was doing, and when he'd be back.

A string of crisp snaps pulled her attention away from her thoughts. Helms was still on the phone, diplomatically brushing off whoever was on the other end of the line. His even pitch never wavered as he flapped a hand toward Leader's door, pantomiming that she should enter. Martinez nodded her head and collected her leather bag, drily adding to her mental list. *LaSalle would never snap at anyone.*

She knocked before opening the door and found the large office much the same as her previous visits. The crystalline white walls sparkled in the artificial light; they were hundreds of feet below the surface, and full spectrum bulbs were as close to natural light as one could get. The subterranean office was cut out of the vast salt deposits underneath Zug Island, and the streaks of pinks, reds, and grays from the mineral impurities gave the otherwise spartan room a touch of whimsy. The only deliberate wall art was Jan Brueghel the Elder's *The Temptation of Saint Anthony*. It was a small piece that hung against a wide white wall, making it feel more like a museum display than office decoration.

The bulk of the space was allocated to filing cabinets, lined up along the back wall behind Leader's desk. Martinez's eye was immediately drawn to the petite woman dressed in a cream cardigan and chestnut corduroy slacks hovering between the desk and the cabinets. Her salt and pepper bob was on the long end and her flipped-up tips swayed as she put away files and retrieved new ones.

At five foot even, any other person of her stature would have been dwarfed by such a setup; Leader was only a few inches taller than the cabinets. But Leader was unlike anyone Martinez had ever met before. Her presence went well beyond the restraints of her physical person. Martinez took a deep breath before speaking. "You wanted to see me, Leader?"

Leader looked over one shoulder and a swish of her bob preceded her hawkish gaze by a millisecond. She had expected the firm knock on the office door, but not an unaccompanied agent. It was yet another small reminder that Helms was assisting her today, along with the mildly disappointing Earl Grey tea and his reflexive habit of calling her Ms. Zervo instead of Leader. She preferred to keep her worlds separate, but minor allowances had to be made in LaSalle's absence. She quickly recovered and swept her arm toward the chairs in front of her desk. "Lancer, please come in and take a seat. I'll be with you in just a minute."

Martinez entered and closed the door behind her, cutting out Helms's smooth voice mid-sentence. She hadn't realized how soundproof Leader's office was until that very moment; although when she really thought about it, she'd never heard LaSalle's voice through the door before, either. While Leader's gaze was elsewhere, Martinez quickly situated herself in an oversized chair, planting her feet solidly on the floor and putting her leather tote beside her to fill the lateral space. In terms of territorial display, it was one of confidence without being aggressive. Finally, she picked a point on the wall and anchored her focus there.

When Leader returned to her chair with files in hand, her keen gray eyes cut across Martinez. Her otherwise conscientious agent had failed to produce a green folder with red lettering from her bag. "Lancer, did you receive a mission brief this morning?"

Martinez felt the weight of the gaze and question and started to sweat a little. "No, just a note informing me of the appointment on top of the dailies," she answered, and rifled through her bag to produce the evidence.

As Leader examined the neat print on the post-it note, Martinez felt the pressure ease a little but dared not relax. Leader pressed the buzzer on the side panel with her other hand. "Ethan, did you send Lancer the file on Lafayette?"

"Yes, Ms. Zervo," he said automatically.

Leader raised her right brow. "To her office on the fifth floor?"

The brief sliver of silence before he answered was the only indication he'd realized his mistake. "No, Ms. Zervo. I sent it to her email."

An email I can't check while I'm in the Salt Mine, Martinez completed the sentence for him in her head. She kept her face still but cringed on the inside for Helms. No one wanted to come up short in Leader's eyes.

"I appreciate the effort to go green, Ethan, but do try to remember the working parameters when you are below ground," Leader commented neutrally.

"Yes, Ms. Zervo. My apologies. It won't happen again," he replied emphatically.

Leader released the button without further comment to her assistant and drily remarked, "Well, that's one mystery solved." The unexpected hint of sarcasm was too much for Martinez and despite her best efforts, the corners of her mouth upturned ever so slightly.

"I'm sending you to Lafayette, Louisiana," Leader announced as she slid her file across the desk to Martinez. "Multiple missing persons case reported last Friday. Your mission is to determine if supernatural forces are responsible."

Martinez opened the dossier and did a quick scan—a wedding gone wrong? That was far from her typical case, which usually started with a dead body. "What brought this to the Salt Mine's attention? Did we get a tip? Or is one of the missing persons someone of interest?" She wouldn't normally have asked questions without having first reviewed the brief, but felt she had some latitude thanks to Helms's oversight.

"No on all counts. One of our analysts spotted it as a suspicious circumstance." Leader sat back in her ergonomic chair and drummed her fingers together, giving Lancer the broad strokes of the incident. "Five women vanished into thin air hours before a wedding, one of which is the event coordinator at the venue and had no personal connection to the wedding party. The bridal suite and reception area were tossed over, but the police found no bodies or blood."

"Unlikely to be a runaway bride or last minute lover's spat," Martinez agreed as she rifled through the images captured at the scene. She paused at the picture of the splattered cake. She had been barking mad before, but never smash-a-cake-into-the-wall mad. "Any witnesses?"

"Not of the damage, but another employee saw a man in the chapel shortly before the police were called. However, they have been unable to identify him, and his description fits no one involved with the wedding or the missing people," Leader patiently fielded questions.

And when things don't make sense, why not magic? Martinez thought to herself as she closed the file. "I'll go over everything in more depth on my way south, but is there anything in here that strikes you as suggestive?"

Leader paused briefly to consider the matter. "The employee that called 911 said she heard music shortly before the screams. And the man she saw in the chapel asked for Pauline, but none of the missing women had that name."

Martinez took a mental note of those two points as she returned the folder to the desk, trusting its duplicate was sitting in her email's inbox. "Parameters?"

"Local law enforcement is at a loss. They haven't found any of the women, dead or alive, and they shouldn't protest too loudly if the FBI stepped in on this one, if you feel that is necessary," Leader qualified.

Martinez nodded. Neither of them wanted to introduce more pretense or paperwork into the process. Her job wasn't to find the missing women, it was to determine if something supernatural was involved and nip that in the bud. However, she liked having options.

"I'll bring my FBI badge just in case, but with no bodies to need access to, I should be able to ascertain if there is anything of interest without it," she stated plainly as she slipped the straps of her bag over one shoulder. "When do I fly out?"

"Ethan should have your travel and lodging arranged, but you might want to confirm that on your way out," Leader added. And then, she sighed so softly that it was almost imperceptible. It may have been the most human thing Martinez had ever seen her indomitable employer do. As she took her leave, it brought an enigmatic smile to her face. Apparently, she wasn't the only one on the fourth floor missing LaSalle.

Chapter Four

Lafayette, Louisiana, USA
30th of January, 9:55 a.m. (GMT-6)

It was balmy 50°F when Martinez left the hotel. While everyone else was bound up in sweaters and winter coats, she was dressed in nothing more than jeans and a short-sleeved shirt, although she had a jacket slung over her bag just in case the weather turned. She chuckled at the couple that passed her at the entrance, commenting on the chilly morning.

As she cleared the front awning, she could feel the sun's warmth on her exposed arms. There wasn't a dot of snow as far as the eye could see. She put on her sunglasses and strolled to her rental—a steel gray Ford Escape.

She'd arrived yesterday evening after two layovers, and Helms had managed to secure her a nice room in an establishment on the upper end of mid-range, the kind that served a hot complimentary breakfast. All that travel time gave her plenty of opportunity to go over the mission brief.

The Salt Mine analysts had put together a collection of articles, social media pages, and a basic bio on each of the missing women. There were no autopsies for them to obtain through the back channels, but they did manage to acquire the initial reports and crime scene photos from the local law enforcement's servers. It was enough to get started.

The bride was Kaylee Parker, a thirty-two-year-old project manager at an oil and gas company. She was the only child of Michael (deceased) and Eileen Parker, who was also among the missing women. According to the engagement announcement in the local paper, she was supposed to marry Leland Kirkwood, a thirty-five-year-old librarian, last Friday in the New Hope Chapel located in the historic Acadian Village.

Their engagement photo was absolutely adorable and utterly predictable. Natural light and a soft lens gave them a glow as they held hands and gazed into each other's eyes in front of a non-descript bucolic backdrop. It was right out of the modern photographer's playbook, indexed under "capturing moments." They seemed happy enough, but didn't everyone in these pictures? How many shots had to be rejected before they got to this one?

If Martinez was reading the subtext correctly, they met via a dating app, and the Salt Mine had them at the same address for the past two years. It was common enough these days, but lust at first swipe didn't have that storybook quality people wanted to project in engagement announcements. They, along with obituaries, were two of the last bastions of traditional newspapers—seeing life events in print still had gravitas among a certain strata of society.

The other two members of the wedding party that had gone missing were Ashley Downer and Mabel Kies, Kaylee's two bridesmaids. The three women had attended the University of Texas at Austin together, and while Downer and Kies remained in Texas, Kaylee returned to her Louisiana hometown shortly after her father passed away. The out-of-towners arrived two days before the wedding and on the surface, they didn't have any local connections except for the bride.

The last missing woman was Eva Chapman, the fifty-eight-year-old event coordinator at LARC's Acadian Village. Native to Lafayette, she lived alone with a blond golden retriever. She had two adult children, neither of whom lived in the state, and she had long been divorced. Her ex-husband had since remarried and had children with his new wife. The analysts weren't able to find any obvious connection between her and the Parkers or Kirkwoods, even though they resided in the same city.

The coworker that called emergency services to the scene was twenty-six-year-old Zoe Miller. Her account of events contained the points of interest Leader had mentioned. The police circulated a sketch of the man she saw in the chapel, along with a description: five-foot-ten, 160-180 pounds, light brown hair, brown eyes, speaks French, last seen dressed in a vintage suit with ruffled collar and top hat. He was labeled a person of interest, but no one had stepped forward with his name or whereabouts.

None of the above had any criminal records, although the older Ms. Parker had a lead foot given the number of speeding tickets she had racked up over the years. There weren't any restraining orders or calls to the police that would suggest a long-standing stalker or harasser. There were no registered magicians among them or in their immediate families.

Martinez had done some remote reconnaissance on the internet last night. Coupled with the information the Salt Mine had provided on the Acadian Village, she had a good lay of the land as she pulled out of the hotel parking lot to follow her GPS out of town. She'd had timed her departure to miss most of the morning rush hour traffic, and it wasn't long until the concrete jungle receded in her rearview mirror.

This region of the Gulf Coast was Cajun country, and Lafayette was the closest thing that passed for the big city in these parts, even though it was only the fifth largest in the state by population. Separated from the rest of the state by the Atchafalaya Basin, it lacked the luster and wealth of Baton Rouge or New Orleans to the east or Shreveport to the north. It wasn't until oil was found in southwest Louisiana that the area caught a break. Money and development flowed in as Cajun families transitioned from working the land to the oil and gas industry.

Lafayette was built on firm high ground—a whole thirty-six feet above sea level!—but just past the rim of the valley lay the wetlands better known as the bayou. Normally a humid and subtropical area teeming with biodiversity, its mild temperatures and low precipitation this time of year made for a pleasant, scenic drive. It wasn't her first choice for a winter getaway, but she wouldn't be too put out if this fishing expedition took a little longer than anticipated. She doubted these parts had ever been touched by a snowplow.

Martinez pulled into the gravel parking lot of the Acadian Village and did a wide sweep until she saw three cars parked on the far side, presumable where the employees parked. Among them, she spotted a silver Toyota Corolla and verified it was the same one registered to Zoe Miller. After she parked the SUV, she did a last minute inventory. Her amber periapt hung under her shirt along with her crucifix and pendant of St. Michael. The former was enchanted, given to her by the Salt Mine to protect her from being targeted by spells, while the latter was mundane, given to her by her mother to guard her body and soul. Her spell-amplifying rosary beads were in one pocket, and a salt-casting vape pen in the other. She tucked her Glock 43 in the hip holster under her shirt along with a magazine of 9mm ammunition and another with banishing bullets. Her FBI badge was in her back pocket, and in her bag were salt replacement packs, gloves, lock picks, sealable plastic bags, and a flashlight.

Martinez slipped on her jacket and hoisted her bag on her shoulder before locking the car. Mobile in hand, she walked up to the ticket office where she could hear someone fussing with something below the counter. "One adult ticket, please," Martinez requested politely to the empty window.

The woman—definitely not Zoe Miller—popped up with a smile and replied, "That will be $8.68 for the self-guided tour." Martinez handed over a ten-dollar bill; she saw little point in leaving electronic proof of her visit until she was certain there was something of interest here, not to mention the 3% surcharge for paying by plastic.

After the attendant made change, she pulled out an inkpad and stamp: an upright alligator wearing a straw hat and playing a fiddle. The pretense of in-and-out privileges amused Martinez as she presented the back of her hand. It wasn't like the security here was watertight.

She followed the winding path deeper into the village, playing the role of tourist while she scanned for signs of security cameras. As soon as she was satisfied there were none, she made a beeline for the Stutes Building. Based on the paucity of cars in the parking lot, she figured this was her best shot at maneuvering with minimal interference.

Outside, the police tape had been removed and there were no work vehicles parked around the perimeter. It was dark inside and when she listened at the door, she heard no noise from within. She donned a pair of gloves before checking the door. It was locked, but she made quick work of it with her picks. She opened the door and slipped inside.

Martinez had her flashlight ready, but instead chose to wait the minute it took for her eyes to adjust to the ambient light dribbling in from the windows. It was a far cry from the crime scene photos—clean up and repair were almost finished. She oriented herself and choose the wall where the cake had been smooshed. If any casting had been done, it would have been there.

She pulled out her vape pen and rotated the end until the notches lined up, engaging the hidden chamber lined with etched runes. After taking a deep breath, she brought the cylinder to her lips and blew out hard. A fine white powder burst out from the aperture and fell to the floor in an even distribution.

Of all the arcane kit Martinez had added to her toolbox in the past year, the saltcaster was by far the most useful diagnostic tool. It was technology created and made portable by Harold Weber, the Salt Mine's resident inventor and quartermaster. By passing regular salt through an enchanted tube, it was able to capture residual magical and display it visually. Not only did it tell her if something supernatural had occurred recently, it produced a unique identifier that could be checked against the Salt Mine's database of magical signatures.

Even when there wasn't an exact match, someone who could read the shapes and motifs might derive some information on what she was dealing with in the field. Martinez still liberally relied on the Salt Mine to interpret the lines and squiggles from the curves and bends, but she was slowly building her literacy in the craft.

Martinez stayed clear of the windows while she waited, intently watching the magically imbued grains. She routinely waited a full minute of no movement before calling it a bust, and she always disturbed the salt to dispel the enchantment afterward, even when there was no change. One had to be careful with magic.

Her patience was rewarded when things started to shift thirty seconds in. No matter how many times she had salted, she still got a small thrill when it started to move—the small proof that magic was real and she had harnessed it hadn't gotten old yet. What seemed like random movement of individual granules would suddenly take shape, like watching a marching band from the stands—one minute, everyone was on foot, but when everyone hit their mark, a pattern would emerge.

She tried to predict its trajectory, but it defied her anticipation—where she expected it to zig, it zagged. She recognized the basic elements that composed the magical signature, but their arrangement and orientation were unlike anything she had seen before. When it was done, the pattern was even more pronounced because the salt had moved the mundane construction dust on the floor in its progression. She snapped a couple of pictures on her phone before kicking the salt and moving on to the bridal suite.

Martinez found the room unlocked, and the scent of lavender assaulted her as soon as she opened the door. The debris was gone and the furniture righted. The suite was once again a calm sanctuary for the bride and her retinue before the hustle and bustle of the actual wedding. She quietly closed the door behind her and cast another round of salt.

She deposited herself onto the chaise while she waited and took in her surroundings. The decor was soft and feminine with ample seating and mirrors, including a full-length tri-fold and a large vanity with a row of bulbs. There were plenty of plugs for charging phones and heating irons, and a line of sturdy hooks were screwed into the wall for hanging heavy dresses. On a dresser was a collection of beauty staples: cotton balls, Q-tips, tissues, bobby pins, hair ties, and a can of hair spray. There was even a small fridge stocked with ice-cold bottles of water.

There were too many floral motifs and pastels for Martinez's taste, but she was hardly the target audience. She harbored no desire to pass herself off as a country girl or southern belle, although she could get used to the chaise lounge. Eventually, the salt shook itself into the same signature that she'd found at the site of the demolished wedding cake. She took another picture, kicked the salt, and reluctantly extricated herself from the low couch.

When she left the bridal suite, she heard the stirring of workmen behind her, preventing her from doubling back unseen. Fortunately, there was another door at the end of the hall that looked like an exit. Martinez quietly crept down the passage and opened the door into a spacious outdoor area topped with trellises. Green foliage wove through the slats and filtered the sunbeams that pierced through the gaps of the swaying canopy overhead. The charm of the softly lit enclave was lost on her; she was focused on getting back to the paved footpath that wound its way through the village. She had one more place to salt.

She stepped out from the wall of greenery and swept the skyline until she found the cross atop the spire of the New Hope Chapel in the distance. "X marks the spot," she drily remarked and started walking in its general direction.

The chapel was empty and quiet when Martinez arrived, and she didn't waste time. According to Miller's statement, the French-speaking man in the fancy dress stood in the vestibule; that was where she cast her salt. The front entry was very dim, making it easy to conceal her true purpose but hard to see if any pattern emerged. Once the salt was out, she rotated the tip of her salt caster, turning it back into a vape pen should anyone find her standing by the doors. Not that she was a smoker—the stuff loaded in the vape pen contained no nicotine, and she only ever puffed on it as a prop during work. Need to return somewhere alone? *Crap, I left my vape pen!* Need to step outside and privately investigate? *I'm just going to grab a quick vape.* Want to butter up a source of information? Join them while they have a smoke. And when she needed to have the salt caster in plain sight? No one questioned why a smoker fiddled with a vape pen.

After a minute, Martinez centered her phone on the ground and took a picture. The camera's flash went off, and on her screen, she saw the same signature as before. She brushed her foot across the salt and went outside to consider her next move.

Something or someone magical was involved in the disappearance of these five women, but to what extent, she did not know. She sent the Salt Mine a quick update and attached the pictures of the signatures for analysis. Things would be exponentially easier if they found a match, and the sooner she got the images in the work queue, the better.

Her next step was ruling out Zoe Miller as the magical signature's owner. She admitted to being at all three locations on the night in question, and there was such a thing as unregistered magicians. If the signature was hers and she wasn't responsible for the women's disappearance, Martinez still had to enter Miller in the Salt Mine's system but Special Agent Martinez could stay out of it and let local law enforcement search for the unidentified man asking for Pauline.

Martinez heard the gaggle of school children come up the path long before she saw them and stepped aside. They were laughing and talking loudly to one another, oblivious to their surroundings in that self-centered way children of a certain age could be. It was a universal constant that kids loved field trips because it got them out of the classroom, and being outside was a bonus—no indoor voices here. Keeping the pack together bore a vague resemblance to a military operation. A tour guide led the charge, their teachers brought up the rear, and parent volunteers patrolled the flank. Martinez smiled at the adults sympathetically and scanned their faces one by one. Alas, no sign of Miller among the bunch.

It wouldn't be hard to find out if she was magically inclined, provided Martinez could get anywhere close to her. Wilson had taught her a few simple parlor tricks and how to modify them so they were only perceived by other casters. If a sudden and startling auditory prestidigitation didn't capture Miller's attention, then Martinez could safely conclude that she was not the owner of the magical signature.

Martinez considered spending more time in the village, but combing its ten acres for one employee sounded too much like searching for a needle in a haystack, especially when there was more than one way to approach the problem.

The parking lot was fuller when Martinez returned to her car, and the silver Toyota Corolla remained in the same spot. If Miller was at work and lived alone, that meant no one was at her apartment right now. Martinez weighed her options against the likelihood of a result and pulled Miller's address off her driver's license. It was certainly worth checking out, and if there was someone home, she was no worse off than she was now.

Generally speaking, Martinez didn't like breaking the law—a byproduct of all those years spent as an FBI field agent. There, process mattered because bad procedure could tarnish or completely negate good results. Better to go through the proper channels, fill out the right forms, and only act within legally specified bounds.

And then she met the devil. Well, a devil—Furfur, Great Earl of Hell to be more precise. He was real, not an allegory or a metaphor but a giant dude trapped in a silver pentagram hundreds of feet below ground. It forced her to reconsider everything she had previous assumed. When hell and all its minions were fact and people could kill someone with magic, what was the point of search warrants and due process if they prevented keeping the real monsters at bay?

Sure, there were still rules and protocols to be followed at the Salt Mine, but they accounted for the supernatural in a way that the mundane world didn't. A little breaking and entering on a Thursday morning didn't even count as a shade of gray if magic was involved in the disappearance of five women.

Miller lived in an apartment complex that clearly had aspirations of being a lifestyle community, but didn't quite hit the mark. It was a gated community, but the front gate was broken and left perpetually open. It had security cameras in plain sight, but anyone who knew how these things worked could tell that they weren't operational. There was a gym, clubhouse, and multiple pools, but they were most likely overrun by the pack of small children that lived in the complex.

It was large enough to warrant a site map to explain the layout, and the units were a cipher of letters and numbers. It took Martinez a few passes to find the right building. There weren't many cars parked in the numbered spaces, which she took as a good sign—most of the residents were away. She pulled into an unmarked spot—being towed for parking in someone's assigned spot was not on today's agenda—and glanced at the windows, noting which had closed curtains and if there was any movement inside the open ones.

The building had an outdoor stairwell in the center, and Martinez took each flight in stride until she came upon Miller's apartment on the third floor. She rang the doorbell and waited. The electronic chime went unanswered; no curious cats came to the window or excited dogs barking or scratching at the door.

She summoned her will and checked for esoteric protections. *Hail Mary, full of grace…* After a cursory sweep, she slipped on a pair of gloves and pulled out her lock picks. The deadbolt yielded after a few delicate jiggles and Martinez was inside.

The living room was well lived in. A colorful crocheted blanket lay disheveled on one side of the sofa with a mountain of pillows stacked against the other. A phone charger dangled over the armrest next to the television remote. The coffee table was covered with clutter: a stack of unopened mail, crumpled take-out bags, an open box of cheese crackers, and an empty ice cream carton with a spoon still inside. On the end table near the phone charger there was a collection of beverage containers, including Styrofoam cups, water glasses, coffee mugs, and wine goblets.

The kitchen was in a similar state. There were dishes stacked in the sink that cascaded onto the counter, and the situation must have been getting dire—someone had eaten cornflakes out of a small metal Ikea mixing bowl with a serving spoon. She did a quick scan of the cupboards for spell components, surprised to find the cans and boxes systematically lined up and organized, but there was nothing arcane within.

She walked down the hall and on her immediate right was a small linen closet with a vacuum cleaner. Further down, the bathroom door was open, and the scent of cucumber and melon body wash wafted into the hall. The towel draped off its edge was still damp. At the end was the hall was the bedroom. The queen-sized bed was covered by shirts and pants still on the hangers. The closet was open and the hamper filled to the brim, tamped down by a bottle of liquid detergent.

Given her options, Martinez elected to cast by the sofa, where Miller had clearly spent a lot of time recently and a little salt would be less likely to draw attention. She fought the urge to tidy while she waited. Just as the minute was drawing to a close, the salt began to move. Usually, the shifting grains would reveal lines, shapes, and patterns, but not this time. The edges of the field contracted, but the salt within retained a uniform distribution. When the salt stilled, it was a perfect circle of white with no contours or detail—a blank magical slate.

Well isn't that interesting? Martinez thought as she snapped a picture.

Chapter Five

Detroit, Michigan, USA
30th of January, 2:25 p.m. (GMT-5)

Beyond the stacks of the sixth floor, the librarians sat behind their circular desk, each with a hot beverage and a stack of books beside them. Their dirty blonde hair was tied back—Chloe's in a braid and Dot's in a low ponytail—and their blue eyes were fixed on their respective tomes.

Joined from torso to hip, they had spent their entire lives at each other's side, Chloe on the right and Dot on the left. Their form of conjunction was the simplest to separate surgically, but they had never seriously considered disunion, although it was mentioned in their more contentious disagreements. The truth was, neither sister could image life without the other, even when the other was being insufferable. It would be like cutting off one's arm; no matter how bothersome or uncooperative it was being, it was still an integral part of you, for better or for worse.

And there were advantages to their situation. Being two minds in one body made it nigh impossible to charm either of them, and they covered twice as much material with their eidetic memories by specializing and coordinating their knowledge acquisition. They always had someone to consult with on difficult matters, and like many twins, they understood each other on a whole other level. As Chloe was fond of saying, two heads were better than one. To which Dot invariably rolled her eyes.

Currently, they were doing some research for Weber, who was itching to tinker with some of the esoteric power generated at the Masonic Temple by the Detroit Roller Derby. The golden circle that the late Sarah Pullman had originally built as a magical bomb had been refitted into a generator. As the skaters made their circuit on the track, their expended will and determination was captured and turned into esoteric energy, which was siphoned off and stored in arcane batteries of Weber's design.

Leader had earmarked a portion for the Salt Mine's reserves, but the rest was allocated to the sixth floor for research and development. While the German engineer daydreamed of applying greater arcane applications to field gear, the librarians were considering all the rituals, spells, and enchantments that had previously been off-limits due to the amount of power it would take to pull them off.

"Oooo," Dot crooned, "how about Eye of the Wyrm?"

"Doesn't that require a scale of an ice dragon?" Chloe gently pointed out. "Where are we going to find one of those? Especially with global warming—"

"Are you sure we don't have any left in cold storage?" Dot grasped at straws. She had always wanted to do that one.

Chloe sighed. Of the two of them, Dot was always the dreamer. "We can check later, but for now, I'll add it to the list of possibilities, contingent on material components." She neatly penned the letters under the heading "Abjuration" and placed an asterisk beside it.

The phone rang and the flashing light indicated the call was coming from the fourth floor. Chloe, who was the designated people person of the pair, picked up. "This is Chloe." Dot heard the voice coming through the line but couldn't make out the words. However, she did discern a change in Chloe's tone. "Of course. We'll take a look at it right away, Ethan."

Dot waited until the receiver was back in the cradle before parroting her sister with exaggerated coquettishness. "Of course. We'll take a look at right away, Ethan. And after that, maybe I could suck your—"

"Dot!" Chloe exclaimed. "I'm just being friendly. LaSalle left big shoes to fill."

"I'm sure you would have no problem helping Ethan fill something…" Dot snidely muttered.

Chloe smiled mischievously as she turned on the monitor and jiggled the mouse. "Would that be so terrible? Ethan's cute."

Dot looked up from her book in disbelief. "A butt chin is not cute."

"It's a dimple that happens to be on his chin," Chloe corrected her, "and I think it looks distinguished."

Dot shrugged to give the impression that she was over it, but she couldn't help herself. "As he gets older, it's going to look more and more like a scrotum." While there was much the sisters shared, the same taste in men was not one of them, and historically, the ones they had agreed upon were never any good for either of them.

"Growing old wasn't what I was planning on doing with him," Chloe playfully replied before turning to serious matters. "Martinez sent in a signature for analysis, and the second floor thinks they may have found a match but they need verification."

"Meh," Dot uttered, which was shorthand for *You've got this, right? Because that sounds totally boring to me. Unless it's something interesting, in which case, you should fill me in.* Chloe waved her hand in reply, which meant *Shouldn't take long.* You keep reading. After a lifetime together, they had cultivated a remarkable efficiency to their communication.

Magical signature analysis had long been automated based on the principles of pattern recognition. As computer technology improved, the Salt Mine had developed algorithms to check for the presence of elements and their relative position to each other. From there, it assigned a percentage of concurrence. Anything below 75% was deemed as not relevant, but anything above that was reviewed by a skilled analyst because there were enough shared features to warrant a closer look. The wheat was separated from the chafe and sent higher up the chain, and Chloe and Dot were the final word in interpreting signatures. It was similar to fingerprints—computers could be helpful in narrowing the search, but it couldn't beat the eyes of a skilled latent print examiner.

As the hard drive woke up from sleep mode, Chloe clicked the Salt Mine intranet icon and opened the awaiting file. First, she looked at what Martinez had sent in: three photos taken in the field at different angles with varying amounts of light. When she was certain that all three were a match to each other, she selected the best one and opened the image from the database, comparing them side by side.

"Well, it is a match," Chloe declared, and Dot filled in *and it's not good news* from her taut enunciation.

Dot put her book down and looked at the screen. It was undead, that much was obvious. The orientation and clustering of the triumvirate scrolls suggested incorporeal. She continued systematically analyzing the signature's components, interpreting them in isolation as well as part of the whole. When she counted the number of branches off the main trunk, she frowned. "Poltergeist." In those three syllables, Dot conveyed her agreement—this was bad news.

Physically speaking, undead came in two broad categories: corporeal and incorporeal. The ones that had physical bodies were solidly present in the mortal realm, although their anti-soul was firmly planted in the land of the dead. They were literally a bridge between two worlds, and severing that connection was fairly obvious: kill the undead. The exact method varied by creature and culture, but speaking practically, one of the Mine's banishment bullets took care of most of the lesser corporeal undead. For the more powerful ones, the sentient ones, it took a little more work to break the anti-soul's connection to the mortal realm.

Incorporeal undead were less straightforward because you couldn't just shoot them. They didn't have a body. Some could even possess people, but killing the vessel didn't eliminate the undead creature from the mortal realm. Additionally, there was more variation in what they could do and how to effectively eradicate a troublesome one.

Poltergeists, like ghosts, were able to manifest in the mortal realm. They could produce sound, knock on doors, open kitchen cabinets, and move other objects of various sizes depending upon individual strength. They tended to do so when no one was looking but were sure to notice. Even the nicest of poltergeists liked to make their presence known. That's how they got their name—German for "noisy ghost."

However, unlike ghosts, poltergeists could physically touch people, and the mean ones had no qualms about biting, pinching, or hitting those that rubbed them the wrong way. The metaphysics behind that behavior was enough to make even the librarians' heads spin. In theory, poltergeists could be appeased, but it was best to expel them altogether because the last thing anyone needed was an angry one hurling knives or physically attacking someone.

"Get word to Deacon," Dot suggested as she returned to her book. "He should have no problem taking care of it." The one good thing about poltergeists was that they were anchored, tied to haunt a location or person. Once you knew you were dealing with a poltergeist and figured out its anchor, it wasn't hard to sever its connection to the mortal realm.

"Oh, it gets better," Chloe ominously informed her sister as she scrolled down the screen where all known encounters were listed. This, Dot could not ignore—she was the dark one, not Chloe—so she joined her in looking at the screen. The signature had four hits in the past two months, all found by Deacon. Her brow furrowed as the implication sunk in. This was Deacon's current white whale, the mobile poltergeist he had been hunting for weeks. "Any bones found?" she inquired.

Chloe opened a different folder in a new window. "Not yet," she answered.

"You better call Leader," Dot advised without a trace of sarcasm or sass.

Chapter Six

Clarence Morris—codename Deacon—climbed the last few rungs and stepped out onto the balcony of the Oak Island Lighthouse. The whipping wind beat against him, depositing fine grains of sand and salt that stuck to the beads of sweat on his ebon brow. He produced a handkerchief from the inner pocket of his camelhair coat and daubed his face and head.

The guide, who had been waiting for him, yelled over the roar. "It's quite a view, isn't it?" She was a compact woman who only came up to his shoulders. Her sable hair was held back in a tight braid and she wore no makeup, which gave him an honest view of her strong features. She was somewhere in her late thirties, maybe early forties by his estimation, and the 131 steps below them hadn't phased her one bit.

"It's breathtaking, almost worth the climb," he replied between panting breaths. He gave her a smile to let her know he was making a joke, which she reciprocated. Unlike the other lighthouses, this one didn't have a winding staircase, but steep ships ladders with eight landings to rest along the way. Morris wasn't exactly in peak physical condition but he'd hustled to save face as the spry younger woman scaled the ladders with ease, all while spouting facts and trivia about the lighthouse and its history.

"Take your time. It's all yours," she assured him. Morris was the only guest in the lighthouse. While the surrounding area was open to the public all year round, it didn't hold regular viewings of the inside until summer. Fortunately, he was able to make an appointment for a private tour at the last minute.

He stepped to the railing and looked down. He was 150 feet in the air and everything looked so small. He panned his eyes out to the water—the choppy waves of the Atlantic resembled Ws scribbled on a child's drawing.

He took in the salty air and eventually regained his breath. Then he centered himself and summoned his will. *I will fear no evil...* The basic shape of his spell congealed, and he started slicing away, pairing it down with economic precision. He had caught glimpses of his quarry in its past works; he didn't need to see everything to know if it had passed this way. He'd save his karma for when it really mattered.

When he was pleased with its shape, Morris closed the loop and let his will flow through the circuit. He put the binoculars hanging around his neck to his eyes and surveyed all with his new gaze. He combed the landscape and the sea, looking for any sign of the poltergeist. He knew it was a long shot, but at this point, that was all he had.

The first disappearance occurred on a lobster boat off the coast of Maine in early December. While they were out at sea, the headcount came up short one deckhand, even though no one had seen him fall in. They started search and rescue efforts and called the Coast Guard to help, but they didn't find him. When the remaining crew pulled up their traps the next day, one of them was filled with the missing man's bones. There was a slapdash attempt at a mundane explanation—the flesh was eaten by a hungry sea—but the Salt Mine knew better. When Morris arrived, he found the magical signature of a poltergeist, performed a ritual on the boat, and put the bones to rest. That should have been the end of the story.

He was then called out to Connecticut a week before Christmas. A canoodling couple last seen at the New Haven Yacht Club Christmas party were reported missing by their respective families. Local authorities searched the area and found what was left of them in a boathouse, tucked into one of the moored rowboats. The cops had plenty of theories of jealous exes and love triangles, but couldn't explain how all that was left was their bones. While others were working on elaborate schemes about how the flesh could have been stripped from the skeletons in a matter of two days, Morris had found the same poltergeist's magical signature again.

By this time, his knew what he was facing, but without knowing where or what the restless spirit was anchored to, there wasn't much he could do but clean up after it, which he did faithfully. Plus, it was still possible that the poltergeist was haunting a person and that could account for its movement across hundreds of miles. He'd put the analysts to work to look for a living connection between the locations and victims and then set his sights to Christmas.

Despite their best efforts, the Mine didn't find a link in their searches, but he didn't have to wait long for another incident, this time in New York. The New Year's Eve fireworks went off without a hitch, but the man in charge of the pyrotechnics on the barge never returned to shore. His bare bones were found the next day, dismembered and shoved down the spent tubes.

No sooner had he finished in New York than the analysts flagged a similar MO in Virginia Beach. An elderly couple stranded along the beach called for roadside assistance, but they were nowhere in sight when the tow truck arrived. Per protocol, the truck driver called their cell phone number to see if they still needed help. When he heard the ringtone in the trunk of their Audi, he pried it open with a crowbar and again, just the bones.

And then nothing—almost a month without new bones. Ironically, Morris found this more disturbing than the eerie placement of the remains. He didn't trust the quiet and was tired of playing whack-a-mole. If this was a new variation of incorporeal undead, Morris needed to get ahead of it. If it wouldn't show itself, he was going to track it down.

Since all the attacks were on or near the ocean, he cooked up a theory that it was using the water to move, similar to how ghosts could travel along ley lines. Nothing else about this restless spirit was standard operating procedure for a poltergeist, so it seemed as good as a place to start as any.

It was moving south along the eastern seaboard, so he took off for the Outer Banks. He was particularly proud of his idea to use the lighthouses as high ground. They dotted the coast with some regularity and were big tourism draws, making them easy to access, even in the off-season. Little was off limits with a bit of persuasion and money, both of which he had in spades.

Oak Island Lighthouse was his sixth stop, well south of the Outer Banks and almost into South Carolina. He made another pass with his binoculars, but it was looking like a bust, just like the others. He dispersed his spell and put the cap back on his binoculars after wiping down the lenses. "Ah, it's beautiful, but I think I'm ready to go back inside," he addressed the woman standing patiently behind him. She nodded and waited for him to begin his descent, allowing her to lock up behind them.

Going down was much easier than the way up, and Morris was able to make small talk. She was former Coast Guard and spent her whole life by the sea. She liked to water ski and ride horses on the beach. And she was single.

When they reached the bottom, he thanked her for the tour and asked where he could get a good plate of raw oysters. Under normal circumstances, he would have asked her to join him, but at the moment, the company of a lovely woman wasn't what he needed—although he hated to let the aphrodisiac effects go to waste.

This case had him flummoxed and he needed to think. He really thought he'd had something with his water theory. If it hadn't come this way, did it make its way inland in Virginia? North America had few ley lines compared to England, but they did exist.

Morris refused to believe the restless spirit had simply given up—that's not how these things worked. Its victims were very random and it was unlikely that a stranded elderly couple was its long-sought-after target. There were incorporeal undead that killed indiscriminately, but those usually haunted specific locations and were not sentient, and Morris was pretty sure this spirit was. There was a twisted humor in where the bones were placed, and it had the good sense to skip over New Jersey and Delaware.

The stark black and white exterior of the Oak Island Lighthouse wasn't much more than a matchstick in his rearview mirror by the time he got back into his rental car. He checked his phone while the engine warmed up: one message from the Salt Mine sent seventeen minutes ago. He wasn't surprised he'd missed the alert over the noise up top and immediately opened the communication. The magical signature in the attached picture was all too familiar to him, and Leader's orders were direct and concise. *Found in Lafayette, LA, bones still not found, Lancer onsite. Liaison ASAP.*

So much for oysters, he sighed. With a few taps of his

thumbs, he responded to the Mine and arranged a flight and the early return of his rental car. Then he sent a message to Martinez with his ETA and a request for her to hold tight until he got there. As he put the car into gear, he shook his head. *It had to be Louisiana…*

*****

Martinez looked up from her phone as the latest cluster of travelers exited the airport. Deacon's flight was supposed to arrive forty-five minutes ago but there had been a delay in Atlanta. She had only met him a few times when a situation required all hands on deck, but he'd made an impression. When she didn't see him, she returned to her reading.

She'd been pleased to hear the analysts had found a match, but it was hard not to feel overwhelmed by all the material they had sent her this afternoon. So far, she'd read over Deacon's reports on the four other cases, as well as Chloe and Dot's primer on undead with an extra section on poltergeists. Currently, she was working her way through the briefs previously provided to Deacon, just in case there was something she found significant in light of what she had seen in Louisiana.

Normally, she would have resisted being taken off lead, but on this occasion, she gladly stepped aside. Deacon was the most seasoned agent at the Salt Mine, and her experience with undead was limited to the Quaker ghosts that lived in her attic. Millie and Wolfhard wouldn't hurt a fly, much less abduct people and leave only their bones. As for poltergeists, her only exposure was the old movie by the same name. Martinez hadn't gotten near a TV for a month after her dad let her watch it; granted, she was only seven at the time.

Martinez put down her phone and rested her eyes after she found herself reading the same paragraph for the umpteenth time. Her brain was fried and she had finished the last of her caffeine half an hour ago. It was dark, and the night was getting its full depth of cold—Louisiana cold, of course, not Detroit cold. She had long turned off the engine and cracked the windows to keep them from fogging, but she needed to stretch her legs and get some fresh air. She took the keys out of the ignition and stepped onto the curb, stretching her calves and working the kinks out of her back. Her mental fatigue improved as the blood started pumping, but it also woke up her belly, which rumbled loudly.

Over the hood, she saw a figure exit a pair of double doors and pegged it as Morris within seconds. He was impeccably dressed in a dark gray herringbone suit under his unbuttoned camelhair overcoat. His leather shoes still had their shine, and the trilby on his head was fashionably notched ever so slightly to one side. He was one of the rare men who could pull off wearing a proper hat, and Martinez would love to see someone try to accuse him of being a hipster. He panned his head from left to right until he caught sight of Martinez flagging him down. He nodded in her direction and rolled his Salt Mine standard issue carry-on beside him as he strode over the crosswalk.

At five-foot-ten and 200 pounds, Morris was what people would euphemistically call husky. His broad square shoulders and large strong hands hinted at the brute he used to be in his youth, but that had been ages ago. What he'd lost to time, he compensated for with charisma. He wasn't traditionally handsome, but there was a grizzled charm in his broad toothy grin. His voice had a timbre that was pleasing to the ear and his deep laugh could be felt as much as heard.

"You have a good flight?" Martinez greeted him and opened the back for his luggage.

Morris shook his head as he stowed his suitcase. "There are no words, but I'm here and that's what counts." He took off his hat before climbing in the passenger seat. There was an effortless ease about him, even though he'd just spent hours on flights and in airports.

Martinez started the car and turned on the defroster. "Have you eaten? I'm starving and there's a chicken place that has those little fried creamed corn nuggets on the way to the hotel."

Morris was black as night and his pearly whites gleamed as he smiled wide. "That is the best offer I've heard all day." As Martinez took the wheel, he sat back and relaxed.

Morris had a love/hate relationship with Louisiana. When he wasn't cursing it, he longed for it. He felt no need to resolve such diametrically opposed urges because both were justified.

It was the land that had borne him, but also abused him. He had no doubt that his life would have turned out differently if he'd hailed from somewhere else, but that choice was never his to make. Regardless of his ambivalent feelings, he could always get behind the food. In spite of everything, it was the only thing that tasted like home.

Martinez didn't jump straight into the case or fill the ride with chatter, and Morris appreciated that. He watched the road roll underneath them in the headlights, and the dark scenery scrolled by in its vast periphery. He didn't realize he'd dozed off until he felt a nudge on his arm.

"We're at the hotel," Martinez informed him when he roused.

"Just resting my eyes," he mumbled as he sat up. As his other senses kicked in, he noted the heavenly smell coming from the paper bucket and sacks. "You already got food?"

"I didn't know what you wanted and just ordered a bunch to go. Figured we'd eat inside while we go over the case," Martinez said, diplomatically alluding to his nap without drawing undue attention to it.

Morris got his room, key card, and wifi password from the woman behind the counter while Martinez took the food to her room, where they had agreed to meet after he'd freshened up. By the time he knocked on her door, it had already been laid out: a ten-piece bucket, two packets of fried corn fritters, coleslaw, greens cooked with bacon, and four biscuits.

"You weren't lying when you said a bunch of food," he teased her as she loaded her plate.

"Better to have too much than not enough, and who doesn't like cold chicken for breakfast?" she asked rhetorically as she pulled her hair back and dug in. Morris silently approved as he filled his own plate; he liked a woman with an appetite.

They didn't talk for ten minutes, each content with devouring their chicken while it was still hot. It wasn't until the eating slowed that Martinez asked him about the case. "So, what's the plan?"

He swallowed the bite in his mouth before answering. "First, we find the bones and put them to rest. The first rule of the undead is don't make more of them." Martinez nodded. She'd read that people killed by an undead creature had a greater likelihood of themselves becoming undead.

Martinez grabbed her sack of corn nuggets and moved from the floor to the sofa—the chicken would keep but it would be a crying shame to let those get too cold. "That sounds reasonable, but the police searched all over the building and the grounds and didn't find anything," she pointed out in case he hadn't fully read the Louisiana brief.

"Ah, but the police were thinking like a human criminal," he countered, waving the half-eaten drumstick in his hand for emphasis. "We need to think like this poltergeist. The bones will be close to where the people disappeared, but hidden somewhere cheeky or audacious. You've walked the scene—any ideas?" He took a hearty bite out of the juicy chicken while Martinez mulled it over.

"If it wasn't smashed against the wall, I would have guessed in the wedding cake," she postulated as she crossed her legs under her. "They would have found the bones during the cleanup and repairs of the reception area and the bridal suite, and there wasn't any furniture big enough to hide five adult skeletons, even if they were dismembered first."

Morris tore off a piece of biscuit to sop up the last bit of greens on his plate. "What about the chapel?"

Martinez smiled as she popped another crispy maize morsel into her mouth. *He has read the brief.* She thought back and scanned her memory. "There is a main altar and side altar. I didn't get a good look at them, but they could be big enough if there is a way to open them."

Morris wiped his hands on a paper napkin before picking up his drink. "Then I suggest we finish eating, put on some dark clothes, and go to church," he declared.

Chapter Seven

Martinez drove past the parking lot of the Acadian Village to check if there were any parked cars. It had closed at four, but there was no way of knowing if it was booked for a private event after hours. After she visually confirmed it was empty, she turned onto the gravel back road that circled around the complex. There was no traffic at this time of night.

There was a mustering yard behind the pavilion, used for loading and unloading trailers and oversized trunks for festivals and concerts. Its location was ideal—it was closer to the New Hope Chapel than the front entrance and not visible from the main road.

She parked the Ford Escape behind a pylon, taking advantage of what cover was available. They exited the SUV quietly. Martinez had her gear loaded in a backpack while Morris opted for his beaten black leather medical bag. "Ready?" she asked in a low voice.

"Lead the way," Morris bid her.

They traveled by moonlight, avoiding flashlight use until

they were inside. It was unlikely there was anyone here to spot the artificial light, but there was no point in trespassing if you were stupid and got caught. Morris kept pace and was surprisingly stealthy and agile for a big guy who claimed to be in his late fifties. Like many of her coworkers, she didn't know Morris's story, but he was quick to identify himself as an old man when it suited him.

When they reached the chapel, Martinez gloved up, took a knee, and picked the lock while Morris covered her. After only a few seconds. Martinez softly grunted as the simple old lock gave way. As planned, they paused long enough for Morris to summon his will and cast the same modified spell from the lighthouse.

Only he could see the haze hanging in the front vestibule. Even in the dark, it glowed a soft magenta. He nodded in affirmation—the poltergeist had definitely been here. He held out his arm, preventing Martinez from walking straight into the metaphysical ether. It was very likely safe, but it was always a good idea to avoid interacting with undead forces so close to the witching hour. She gave him a quizzical look but mimicked the wide berth he made on his way to the sanctuary.

Everything was the same as this morning, but it looked eerie in the dim moonlight coming in through the windows. The large wooden cross hanging above the main altar drew Martinez's eye. It was simple, unadorned by the image of a crucified Christ, but the stark contract against the white wall spoke volumes.

Like the rest of the chapel, the altar was white and modest in shape and decoration. There were few embellishments to break its clean lines, and the only splash of color was a trace of gold outlining the arches. A brass lectern sat on top, there to hold the word of God, with four candlesticks spread across its length.

They walked up the center aisle, avoiding the bank of windows on either side. A series of small wooden plaques lined the front. Martinez shined her flashlight at one of them: a carved relief of Jesus on the ground, his third fall based on the adjacent scenes. The ninth station, something deep inside her repeated past teaching—neglected knowledge but not forgotten.

The practice of remembering Christ's final days as a man on earth wasn't exclusive to Catholics, but they took it to a whole new level, codifying fourteen distinct steps that started with being condemned by Pontius Pilate and ended with being laid in the tomb. Collectively, they became the *Via Crucis* or the Stations of the Cross. Protestants kept the general practice but changed the terminology to the Passion of Christ.

The idea was if people really understood how horrific his last days were, it would bring more people to the faith. See what God's son went through to save you? Unfortunately, it was often used to fetishize the gruesome details and really lean into the gore, all in his name.

Martinez had been raised a good Catholic, baptized at birth and attended parochial school until college, but she'd left all that behind her as soon as she was on her own. Even when her mother was still alive, she was more of a Christmas and Easter Catholic. Just looking at the stylized panels reminded her of reciting the devotions during Lent and on Good Fridays at Sacred Heart. To this day, she refused to wear anything plaid.

"I don't see any doors or panels," Morris spoke in a low voice.

Martinez turned her attention away from the plaques and onto the altar. "That's because it's plaster." She ran her beam and hands along its surface. "The bones can't be in there. There's no way to put them inside without damaging it."

"Anything is possible with the supernatural," he remarked and gently tapped a knuckle against it: it resonated. "It's hollow, and if the bones were completely encased, I wouldn't be able to see anything from the outside."

Martinez felt ill at ease. She was a lapsed Catholic, but not that lapsed. "I'm not saying no, but can we at least take a look at the other altar before we deface this one?" she negotiated.

"Sure," he agreed. It was a reasonable request, and he was nothing if not a reasonable man.

The side altar was wooden, with a depiction of the Last Supper carved in the panels. There were no obvious doors or hinges, but as they moved closer to examine it, Morris saw a faint line of magenta in the wood. "I've got something over here." He traced the seam with his gloved hand and tried to pry it open without any luck. "It's stuck," he reported.

"Or locked," Martinez replied as she ran her fingertips across the etched wood front. "I found a key hole. Hold the light for me?"

Morris held the beam true while Martinez went to work with her lock picks. One by one, the sticky tumblers fell into position, and she felt the lock release a fraction of a second before Morris heard it click. "Ready?" she asked Morris.

He put his leather bag down on the front pew and withdrew a large silver cross. "Open it."

Hail Mary, full of grace... she summoned her will and opened the door. The entirety of the space was filled with bones, neatly stacked from top to bottom. It was impossible to tell if all of the missing women were here at first glance, but five skulls were set in the wall of bones. In front of the central skull was a diamond engagement ring.

A wall of anguish hit Martinez, like standing knee deep with her back to the ocean and getting slammed by an unseen wave. She kept to her feet as it rolled off her esoteric protections, but they only lessened the impact. Tears started to well in her eyes and she stepped back, putting distance between her and the remains. She took a seat on a pew and grabbed the rosary in her pocket.

This pain was nothing new to Morris. It was the agony of a life cut short without mercy or compassion, times five. He did not fear or shun it; instead he was humbled by it. He stepped up and took its measure. "You think you could lock this thing up again?" he asked Martinez.

She discreetly wiped her eyes and regained her composure. "Sure," she replied, staring at the macabre scene. "The mechanism is stiff but not seized."

"Then it's time to put these poor souls to rest," he said resolutely. He extracted his tools from his bag and laid them out on the pew: a candle in a tall glass jar, a box of long matches, a small brass bell, and a slim strip of white cloth with blue strips running perpendicular to its length. He lit the candle with a long match and set it on the floor a few feet away from the altar. Then he unwrapped the dampening cloth from clapper of the bell.

"No matter what happens, don't put yourself between me and them," he instructed Martinez. Normally, he would have made this a learning opportunity for a newer agent, but it was too dangerous with this many souls. "Do you understand?"

Martinez dumbly nodded her head. "I need you to say it out loud," he insisted. All traces of his laid-back demeanor were gone.

She repeated his words. "No matter what happens, I won't get between you and them."

Satisfied, Morris centered himself. *I will fear no evil…* He rang the bell, and the single chime filled the whole chapel. Martinez couldn't imagine any other sound existing until its peal had dissipated.

He stood in front of the open altar, cross in his hand, and spoke his will. "You are no longer flesh. You are no longer bound to your pain." Even though he was speaking at a normal volume, it vibrated with authority and Martinez felt its echo in her chest.

"Let this fire burn the horror of your death. Do not carry it with you. It will bring you no joy," he commanded. The flame flickered and bounded above the height of the jar, like adding fuel to a fire. The flame lurched progressively higher until it was four feet in the air. Each surge generated an unseen energy that saturated the air, causing the hairs on Martinez's arms to stand on end.

After the fifth leap of the flame, Morris's voice turned tender, although no less commanding. "Your death has not gone unseen. Cling no more to this place. It is time to go home." A gust of wind appeared out of nowhere and flew around the chapel. Martinez didn't know if it was a byproduct of all that pent-up energy or if the owners of the bones were not going to go quietly. She held on to her rosary and said a Hail Mary, bracing herself for whatever was next. It didn't bother her that this wasn't a Catholic place of worship because she wasn't praying.

Morris stood his ground and held his cross tightly. His other hand was placed across his chest and the ends of his prayer shawl flapped in the gale. He'd done this enough times to know the difference between bluster and defiance. He spoke again, but this time gentler, "Your time has come. Be at peace."

Martinez could still hear his soft words laced with magic despite the whipping wind. The roar was loudest right before all the air rushed out of the room. In an instant, the high flame sunk back into the jar. She didn't know where the wind had gone—none of the windows or doors were open. She held her breath, not knowing if there was anything left should she try to take another.

Morris stood immovable as the chapel fell silent and empty. He scanned the bones and saw all the taint gone. He rang the bell once more. This time, its volume was small but its tone still true. His work was done.

"It's over," he said for Martinez's benefit, who was still plastered in the pew by the catharsis that had just blown by. His voice pulled her back to the here and now, and she suddenly remembered to breathe. She inhaled sharply and turned her flashlight to the side altar. All that remained of the flame was a trail of thin black smoke drifting up from the spent wick.

She spoke as she rose from the pew, mentally dusting herself off. "Right, I'll just lock this back up." Martinez approached the altar carefully, poking it with her will—not that she didn't trust Deacon, but better to be safe than sorry. When she perceived that whatever was there before wasn't there now, she dismissed her will. Flashlight in mouth and lock picks in her hands, she set the tumblers back in the locked position while Morris backed his gear, arranging everything just so in the well-worn leather bag.

She tugged gently on the panel to make sure it was locked and slung on her backpack. "Done and dusted. Not bad for a night's work."

Morris grabbed his bag and ushered her down the aisle toward the exit. "We'll have the Mine call in a tip. Tomorrow, we start tracking down this spirit."

Chapter Eight

Lafayette, Louisiana, USA
31ˢᵗ of January, 6:45 a.m. (GMT-6)

Zoe Miller woke up with a smile on her face. There were no screams or cries for help that needed to be drowned out with the white noise of the TV, no kaleidoscope of pain spinning in her dreams, and no fear lurking in the quiet moments. She had slept through the night, the first time in days.

All week long, her unconscious mind kept replaying the scene in the chapel, try as she might to forget. It was worse in her sleep when her brain took liberties with reality. When she'd consulted the internet, the consensus was mild post-traumatic stress, which seemed weird to her. She had witnessed no violence nor was she violated. At the time, she didn't even feel in danger and the man in the chapel was nothing but polite. It was only later that she realized what could have happened—but for the grace of God, she too could be missing.

She didn't know if it was possible to be traumatized by something that didn't happen, but if she had PTSD, she was more inclined to believe it was from being questioned by the police. As a young woman of color, she steered clear of law enforcement, but when five people disappear, there was no avoiding them.

She reached over the armrest for her phone and switched off the alarm. Still half asleep, she left it plugged in and charging while she did some light surfing. She liked a few photos and watched a super cute dog video that made her laugh. She replied to a DM that came in after she had already gone to bed, albeit in emojis because it was too early for words. As she fully roused, she checked in with herself. She was still worn down, but was no longer bone tired. It was amazing what a good night's sleep could do.

When she sat up, she saw the mess around her for the first time. She asked herself how she had let things get so bad on her way to grab a trash bag from under the kitchen sink. When she saw the tsunami of dishes that had taken over, she was utterly appalled. Zoe readily admitted she was not a neat freak, but she wasn't a slob either.

One thing at the time, she told herself as returned to the living room and threw away the empty food containers. She shook out the blanket and a rogue Cheez-It fell out. She bent down to pick it up and found salt spilled all over the place. *How on earth did that happen?* She added the stale cracker to the trash and vowed to vacuum this weekend. She neatly folded the throw and arranged the pillows, transforming the makeshift bed back to a couch. She surveyed her progress and deemed it a good start.

She re-entered the kitchen and ignored the dishes long enough to rummage for food. Sleeping through the night meant no late night snacking and she was actually hungry this morning. One look in the fridge told her she needed to grab breakfast on her way to work, and it was probably a good idea to stop by the grocery store on her way home. Not that she had anything clean to cook on or eat out of.

Realizing her dilemma, Zoe quickly packed the dishwasher like a three dimensional puzzle. There was more need than rack space, but at least the remaining dirty dishes now fit in the sink. She loaded the liquid detergent but thought better than to start it this early in the morning. This was the nicest apartment complex she had ever lived in, but even here, the walls carried the vibrations of machinery extraordinarily well. She set the timer to start in two hours, when most of her neighbors would be awake if not at work. She fought the urge to continue cleaning now that she could actually see the counters, remembering she had to get ready for work.

With Eva gone, everyone at LARC had pitched in to pick up the slack, but there wasn't a lot of staff at the Acadian Village in the first place. On top of routine duties, someone had to deal with the police, organize the cleanup, and figure out what bookings were on the horizon. In Eva's absence, her boss had been around a lot more. While Zoe was glad she hadn't been asked to bat out of her league, his presence was disruptive to her flow and she'd taken to coming in early so she could work n peace.

His frustration was understandable. Like anyone who had been at their job a long time, Eva had her own system for keeping track of clients and contractors. She had a rolodex of names and numbers, but there was a plethora of information she never bothered to write down or excise because they were things she already knew—which caterers were kosher, which vendors to use for tables and chairs for indoor events versus outdoors, which florists were reliable, and which businesses had gone under. And heaven help anyone who tried to decipher her personal brand of shorthand in her calendar. When her boss was there, Zoe could hardly go more than thirty minutes without being interrupted by questions she didn't know the answers to either.

After Zoe used the toilet, washed her face, brushed her teeth and fixed her hair and makeup, she went to her bedroom to get dressed. She made an outfit out of what clean clothes she had left, but it was slim pickings. She cut eyes at the hamper and spied the bottle of detergent she had put on top to remind herself to do laundry this weekend. Of all the domestic tasks, she found laundry the worst.

Once she was dressed, she rifled through an old cigar box that acted as a jewelry box. She always wore the same necklace—a locket her grandmother had given her on her sixteenth birthday—but she liked to change up her earrings from time to time. She stopped when she found the scalloped earrings Eva had given her two Christmases ago.

Since her disappearance, Zoe had thought a lot about Eva. The older woman had taken her under her wing when she'd arrived in Lafayette with next to nothing. The hurricane and prolonged flooding had taken everything, including her mémé, and when things didn't get better after a couple of years, she couldn't stay there with the memories any longer. Though Eva wasn't a relation, she'd become the closest thing Zoe had to family. She would check on her when she was sick, caution her against getting involved with the wrong sort of men, and brought her homemade goodies on a regular basis. That woman could bake like nobody's business.

Last night she'd even dreamt of her. Zoe was at work in the administration office and Eva stopped by with a box of cookies. The two of them were chatting over coffee and sweets like they had done so many times before. It felt so real but even in the moment, Zoe knew it had to be a dream because Eva was still missing.

Then Eva pulled a non sequitur. "You know, even though I don't get to see them as much as I would like, I'm really proud that my kids got out of Louisiana and found their own way. They know I love them, but I don't think I've ever told them that. If you see them, will you let them know?"

"Why don't come back and tell them yourself?" Zoe playfully chided her, but instead of returning sass in kind, Eva became very serious.

"Will you do it? For me."

"Of course," Zoe readily agreed. She didn't understand what was happening, but there was nothing she wouldn't do for Eva.

Eva's body relaxed and she was back to her old self. "Good. Then I better get going before we both get canned. They don't pay us to sit around and eat cookies."

Zoe objected. "Can't you stay a little longer?" She had the inextricable notion that if she let her go, she would never see her again.

Eva smiled radiantly. "No, sweetie. I have to go, but you take care of yourself." She gave her a big hug and just like that, she was gone.

Zoe stared back at her reflection and fought back the welling tears with deep breaths. In through the nose, out through the mouth. She waved her hand in front of her face, trying to fan away the tears and sadness. *Not now*, she told herself. She didn't have time to redo her makeup.

Once the moment passed, she unhooked the earrings' clasps and slid them through her earlobes before relocking them. She shook her head side to side and watched them dangle in the mirror. Eva always had good taste.

Zoe slipped on her shoes and did her routine check before leaving the house: phone, wallet, keys. She grabbed the bag of trash and put it in the dumpster on the way to her car. Her silver Toyota Corolla wasn't sexy, but it was the first new car she had ever bought, which made it precious.

She stopped at the drive-thru and treated herself to an egg and sausage croissant sandwich and a fancy beverage that was more sugar and whipped cream than coffee. She had been in a funk all week, and the idea of a little treat lifted her spirit.

She was singing along to the radio when she pulled into the Acadian Village parking lot. She stopped mid-chorus when she saw the empty squad car parked next to her boss's car. "What now?!" she groaned in the sanctuary of her Toyota as the singer continued without her.

There was no one manning the front entrance at this early hour, and Zoe went straight into the village, following the path to the dentist's house. The door was unlocked and she prepared herself for an encounter with her boss and the police. Instead, she found the office empty.

She went to her desk and turned on the computer before unwrapping her breakfast and taking a bite. It was still warm, and the greasy sausage was distinctly different but complimentary to the fluffy scrambled egg and the buttery flake of the croissant. *Today, there is no such thing as calories*, she declared as she sipped her warm beverage.

She didn't see the post-it note on her monitor until she sat down at her desk, but she recognized the messy print as the same hand that signed her paychecks. *Chapel—keys to the altar?*

"There are no keys to the altar," she answered the scrawled query out loud. She put her sandwich down and checked the keys cupboard: nada. She looked at the charge station and found all the walkie-talkies docked. Zoe ruefully sighed. *So much for finishing the weekly reports this morning.*

No one would blame her for taking five minutes to finish her breakfast, especially since she'd arrived forty-five minutes early, but she could just see her boss trying every key on the giant ring before he figured it out. She wrapped up her food to keep it warm and headed for the chapel.

Chapter Nine

Lafayette, Louisiana, USA
31st of January, 7:25 a.m. (GMT-6)

Martinez woke to a buzzing and when she didn't find her phone on the nightstand, she frantically searched the sheets. "Hello?" she groggily answered the call.

"Have you had breakfast yet?" Morris cut to the chase.

Martinez rolled over and checked the time on the small digital hotel clock. Normally by this time, she would have done her calisthenics, showered, dressed, and been halfway through a piece of cold chicken and a cup of hot coffee. But when the alarm sounded at six, she was having none of it and went back to sleep. "Not yet, but we have plenty of time," she assured him. "Breakfast is open until nine."

Martinez gathered he didn't think much of the hotel's complimentary fare by the severity of his tut. "How does a real breakfast sound?" he suggested.

She relished the idea of staying in bed a little longer—she so rarely slept in—but she wanted to hear her options. "What did you have in mind?"

"I know a place, but you have to drive. My treat," he

offered.

She lazily stretched out and yawned while she thought it over. "Sure. Give me twenty minutes."

"All right, but don't sneak in any cold chicken. The food will be worth the wait," he promised.

Martinez smiled. "Sounds good. Meet you in the lobby?"

"I'll be the well-dressed one waiting," he signed off.

Reluctantly, Martinez started pulling herself together and flung the sheets back. She couldn't understand why she was so wiped. It wasn't like she'd powered the ritual last night. She was just a spectator and all her will went into basic protections. Nevertheless, she had just crashed after they got back to the hotel and put in a request to the Mine to have someone make an anonymous tip.

Fortunately, she could do her morning ablutions, hair, and makeup on autopilot. As for attire, the choice was simple. She pulled out the navy suit hanging in the closet—they were going in as FBI as soon as they got word and she needed to look the part.

She entered the lobby with a minute to spare and found Morris chatting with another guest, an elderly woman with thick glasses sharing a laugh with him. He was back to his gregarious self this morning, although Martinez could now pick out hints of what lay behind the good humor. Keys in hand, she approached the pair. "Ready for breakfast?" she asked neutrally, uncertain of what tale he'd spun for his interlocutor to amuse himself.

"Always. You don't get to look like me skipping breakfast," he said with a self-deprecating smile. "Thank you for keeping me company, Ms. Emmagene."

"It was nice talking to you, Mr. Maycotte. You two enjoy your breakfast," the septuagenarian cooed. He tipped his hat, and she was still grinning when they left her to her cup of coffee.

Deacon preferred to work in the shadows, but when he needed to be seen, he became Charles Maycotte, consultant for the FBI. He didn't have the experience or procedural knowledge to pass himself off as a G-man, but he was intimately familiar with human psychology and all the terrible knots it could tie itself into.

The plan was straightforward. An untraceable anonymous tip would lead local authorities to the bones, which would be enough to warrant the FBI's arrival to make inquiries and ascertain if this case was connected to the other murders along the eastern seaboard. Given the grotesque details, no one would question why Special Agent Martinez brought a profiler. They just had to give it time to percolate.

"What's the name of this place?" Martinez asked Morris once they were in the car.

"It doesn't really have a name," he replied as he tugged on the seatbelt. "It's just a place locals go to get good food."

Phone in hand, Martinez tried a different tactic. "Okay,

what's the address? For the GPS."

Morris smirked. "Just drive. I'll tell you where to go."

On the whole, the GPS was much better at giving anticipatory guidance, but it was not nearly as entertaining as Morris's directions. *Go straight past the Chicken Shack. Veer right at the fork in the road—no, more right. Take a left at the stuffed gorilla. Oh, we should have turned right back there—circle back around.* She wouldn't recommend it for general use, but it was fine for taking the long route to breakfast.

"This is it," he announced as Martinez took her final turn into a lot with a rundown building in the back. There were no delineated parking spaces, so Martinez pulled parallel to another vehicle, giving it plenty of lateral space to avoid dings. Rental car companies were brutal about that sort of thing.

A small brass bell attached to the front door rang as Morris opened it for her; and it was like stepping back into another time. The linoleum floor was black and white harlequin and the tables were covered with white and red-checkered oilcloth. Along the far wall was a counter with a line of stools bolted to the floor. A short ledge ran flush for the parties of one to rest their feet.

A lone waitress behind the counter was topping off coffees. If she'd been wearing a pink uniform with white trim and a nametag, Martinez would have chalked this up as a retro throwback. Since she was wearing jeans and a knit top, Martinez guessed this place just hadn't changed much over the decades.

"Take a seat where you like. I'll be with you in a second," the waitress greeted them before disappearing into the back through a swing door. Martinez selected a table in the corner, eying the full pie case on the way. There were a few people at the counter, and a group of three older men sat at a table at the other end of the room. The suited pair stuck out like a sore thumb, but the other patrons paid them no mind beyond stolen glances upon entry.

It was definitely an eatery, but calling it a diner was a little generous. It was the kind of establishment that didn't need to print a menu because everything fit on a chalkboard, priced à la carte. It reminded Martinez of the numerous taquerias she had eaten at over the years. The selection may not have been broad, but what they did, they did well. The smell of fresh coffee was enough for her to give it a shot.

The waitress returned from the back bearing a plate of food from the kitchen: fried eggs and bacon accompanied by a pair of fluffy, golden biscuits. She set it down on the counter along with a wire rack of sweet, savory, and spicy condiments. The grateful man liberally dosed it with Tabasco before digging in, which made her smile. She liked people who enjoyed their food.

True to her word, she made her way to their table and put down two sets of utensils, each wrapped in a paper napkin. "What can I get ya'll to drink?"

"Coffee for me," Martinez answered.

"Same as the lady," Morris seconded.

"Ya'll take cream?" she asked.

"If it's no trouble," he replied.

At that she took note—manners were a dying breed. "No trouble at all. Be right back."

She slid back behind the counter and performed a series of movements she'd done over and over, a well-rehearsed server's ballet. She grabbed two clean mugs from the crate and slung them on the last three fingers of her left hand. She grabbed a stainless steel cup with her left thumb and index finger; it was still cold to the touch. Then she grabbed the coffee pot from the burner plate and headed out.

"Here's the cream," she explained as she set the steel cup down next to the fluted glass sugar pourer. Once she could rest the mugs on the table, she unthreaded her fingers from the handles and filled them up, leaving room on the top. "And there's your coffee. Do ya'll know what you want to eat, or do you need some time?"

Martinez tilted her head to the side and looked at Morris. "You order for us. I picked dinner last night." Her delivery was straight but the word choice was a little more evocative than she intended. Morris let it slide; he was accustomed to bringing out the mischief in everyone.

"A platter of fried oysters, a bowl of cheesy grits, and biscuits with sausage gravy topped with two fried eggs," he ordered without having to think about it. "And can you bring some extra plates so we can share?" The waitress didn't write it down; she had a memory like an elephant.

"How you want those eggs?" she quizzed him.

"Firm whites, runny yolks," he answered automatically, as if there was any other way to fry an egg.

"Coming right up," she said with a smile. If it was a test, Morris had passed. She sauntered back to the swinging door and notched it open with her hip. "Crispy pearls, extra grits, and runny frog eyes with a squeal."

Martinez poured a little sugar and a splash of milk in her cup, uncertain of portion size in the absence of packets and little plastic cups. "How did you ever find this place?"

"A recommendation from a hotel receptionist long ago," he replied as he opened the flip-top lid of the steel cup and doled out a generous amount of milk for the size of the mug. "The locals always know the best places to eat, but you have to ask the older ones. Young people don't know," he sagely imparted wisdom as he stirred in some sugar.

"That's borderline ageist," Martinez cautioned him. She considered herself youngish and definitely knew about good food.

"It may be, but that doesn't mean it's wrong," he asserted before taking a sip. "Even the coffee's good here."

"It's the chicory," she stated knowingly to further discredit his theory. "And it should be, with as much sugar and milk as ou put in. It's paler than your coat."

He pish-poshed her remark and changed subjects. "Tell me what we know about the witness."

Martinez had requested more background information on Zoe Miller after she'd salted her apartment, and started with the broad strokes. "Zoe Miller, twenty-six years old, originally from New Orleans's Ninth Ward but settled in Lafayette five years ago. Lost almost everything in a hurricane two years before that, including her grandmother who raised her after her mother's death. Has an associate's degree in accounting and has been working at Acadian Village the last four years. No criminal record—not even a speeding ticket. She's not registered as a magician and there were no signs of casting or even protective charms in her apartment."

"Yet she saw our spirit—spoke to him even—and lived to tell the tale," he puzzled. "I find that very curious."

Martinez opened her phone and pulled up a picture. "This is what came up when I salted her apartment. I've never seen anything like it. Is it possible for saltcasters to misfire?" she postulated.

He cut his eyes at her. "Don't let Weber hear you say something like that." He leaned forward to take a better look. "That's not what this is. Ms. Miller isn't a practitioner, but she has the ability to become one."

Martinez gave him a skeptical look. "I thought magicians had their power come in during adolescence, along with acne and growth spurts."

"Not everyone with the aptitude to practice magic actually learns how, either because they didn't know or the decision was made not to develop it. Take yourself, for example. You didn't start until you were well into adulthood."

She was genuinely surprised by his point, even though it was completely logical. The truth was, she was so used to thinking about magicians as something "other" that she hadn't considered her own abilities as part of the same phenomenon. When she'd signed on at the Salt Mine, a whole other world opened up and in the rush, she'd never thought to ask why she could cast. She'd just assumed it had something to do with Chloe and Dot helping her.

The magical signature she had come to recognize as her own had a form, but perhaps that was not always so. She was well into magical training when she'd had the ability to salt herself. Was that how Leader found her for recruitment? Was one of the numerous cases she'd worked as an FBI field agent suspected to be supernatural in nature and a Salt Mine agent picked up her blank signature inadvertently? She'd not bothered to ask such questions when she signed on; she was never one to dwell in the past once a decision had been made.

Although it raised other questions. If her abilities were a dormant predilection, that would mean someone in her family was likely a magician, or at least could have been. She could see her devout Catholic mother suppressing such things because hey smacked of witchcraft, but she could also believe her abuela knew how to cast and ward off an evil eye. Maybe, like red hair, magic was recessive and could skip a generation, which would explain why old magical families were so particular about breeding.

Her brain flooded with these possibilities, but all that came out of her mouth was, "Huh, I hadn't thought of it like that."

Despite her attempts to conceal it, Morris could tell his comment stirred muddy waters. "We'll know more when we interview her," he remarked and redirected her focus on the case. "Let's go over her statement of events one more time."

Chapter Ten

Lafayette, Louisiana, USA
31st of January, 6:15 p.m. (GMT-6)

What had started as such a promising day took a sharp turn after the locksmith drilled out the altar's lock and the stacks of bones were found within. By that time, Acadian Village had opened, and all the visitors had to be found and escorted out. The wedding scheduled for the chapel tomorrow afternoon had to be canceled with much consternation and gnashing of teeth, but there was nothing to be done about it. The New Hope Chapel had become an active crime scene packed with human remains.

Within an hour of discovery, the crime scene investigators had descended upon the chapel. Zoe had no idea how long it would take to remove all those bones, much less reassemble them and determine which femur belonged to whom. The police had commandeered the administration office to interview the staff. By noon, everyone had been sent home for the weekend. She'd been thinking of taking some time off, but this was not what she'd had in mind.

As soon as she got home, Zoe started cleaning. She finished

what she started in the kitchen, putting away the clean dishes and loading the machine for round two. Once she had an empty sink, she wiped down the counters and mopped the floor. The astringent scent of pine hung heavy in the air.

Then she moved on to the bathroom. She cleaned the bathtub and sink, scrubbed the toilet, Windexed the mirror, and mopped that floor, too. When all was white and the chrome sparkled, she pulled out the vacuum, going over every surface of the apartment including the baseboards, crown molding, and window treatments. She even dusted beforehand, which was generally against her religion.

In the bedroom, she put away her clean clothes and tackled the laundry, sorting the whites from the colors from the delicates. She stripped the bed sheets and put on new ones, adding to her laundry pile, but what was one more load at this point? There was order and purpose in the doing, and she took comfort in the smell of bleach and detergent. All things must be cleaned.

As long as she kept moving, she could push reality back for a little while longer—Eva was no longer a missing person, but a pile of bones. Of course, the police hadn't yet officially identified the remains by the time she'd left work, but she didn't need dental records to know Eva was among them. She knew it in her heart. Why else had Eva visited her last night in her dreams? Even in death, she was watching out for Zoe, preparing her for what was to come.

When there was nothing left to clean and the third load of laundry was rolling in the dryer, Zoe sat in her immaculate living room and cried. There was no need to spare her makeup now.

She supposed she should eat something, but she never made it to the grocery store. She didn't even have milk and butter to make a box of macaroni and cheese, and she hadn't sunk low enough to use the cook water to make the sauce. She pulled out her phone and trawled the internet for coupons on something that delivered. She didn't have it in her to leave the house tonight. While she waited for her order, she turned on the TV to keep her company.

She was folding warm laundry and watching game shows when a firm knock fell on her door. She didn't think twice about opening it, but instead of orange beef and hot and sour soup, she was greeted by two people in suits.

A tall Latina woman in a navy suit stepped forward and pulled out a thin leather wallet. "Good evening. I'm Special Agent Martinez of the FBI and this is my associate, Mr. Maycotte. We are looking for Zoe Miller."

Zoe's mind raced as she took a hard look at the presented identification, even though she had no idea what to look for. *FBI! Will this day never end?* She regained her poise and responded without moving from the doorway. "I'm Zoe Miller. May I ask what this is about?"

"We wanted to speak with you about recent events at the

Acadian Village," Martinez replied as she tucked her ID back in the inner pocket of her jacket.

"But I've already told the police everything I know," the young woman wearily protested.

Martinez stayed firm. "Ms. Miller, the local authorities have confirmed that the three missing local women were among the bones. They're still waiting for confirmation on the other missing persons visiting from out of town. We've been called because this is now a murder investigation that bears a striking resemblance to recent murders that have occurred in other states."

Zoe was visible disturbed by the news. "There are others?"

"In Maine, Connecticut, New York, and Virginia," Martinez ran down the list. "Eleven dead people in total, and you are the first witness we have that could lead us to who is responsible." Martinez threaded her words with a little magic. "We just need a little bit of your time, and then you can get on with your weekend." She let her spell settle and do its work while Zoe hemmed and hawed at the door, crossing one foot behind the other. Zoe didn't love talking to police, but these two didn't make her feel anxious like the other cops. Plus, she didn't want her neighbors to see the FBI hanging around her door.

"I suppose you can come in," Zoe relented.

When she entered, Martinez could hardly believe it was the same apartment she'd salted just yesterday, but the place did reek of disinfectants. Zoe hastily removed the laundry from the couch, stuffing her underwear under other articles of clothing before putting the full basket on the floor. "Sorry, I was in the middle of laundry. Please, take a seat." She turned off the TV and took a seat on a chair next to the couch. "What do you want to know?"

Martinez sat furthest away, letting Morris take the lead. That was the plan: she'd get them in and cover his back while he'd work his skills.

"Ms. Miller, I'm trying to build a profile of who it is that's doing all this. I'd like to hear about the night you encountered the man in the chapel, the one that spoke French to you. In your own words, in your own time." His voice was like velvet, lush and soft. Zoe's heart rate slowed and she breathed a little easier.

"Well, it's just like I told the police. I was in the chapel going over everything before the wedding. I heard someone behind me ask '*Où est Pauline?*' Based on the way he was dressed, I assumed he was part of the wedding and gave him directions, in French, to where the bridal party would be. He left and I never saw him after that." Zoe was concise and to the point—the sooner she was done with cops and the FBI, the better.

Morris adjusted his pitch slightly and tried again. "Was is French or Cajun?" Although Cajun had its origins in French, time and isolation had changed it to the point where it was lmost unintelligible to straight Francophones.

Zoe smiled at the question and all that it said in the asking. "It wasn't a long conversation, but the patois was definitely more French than Cajun." He smiled back, like they were sharing a private joke.

"Tell me more about his clothes," he invited her to expound. "The police report was very vague on the details, just called them 'vintage.'" Morris wasn't too concerned about fashion; what he needed was time to feel out Miller, preferably while her mind was focused on something else. In his experience, women could talk forever about clothes.

Morris hung on her every word, spinning his spell into a delicate lace. The more intently he listened, the more she spoke. She had just gotten to the gentleman's footwear when Morris felt something, a slight resistance against one of his arcane threads.

"What was it that you found strange about his shoes?" he asked inquisitively. Martinez said nothing about the randomness of the question, and Zoe was so into the connection Morris had established between them that she didn't even think to wonder how he knew such things. She certainly hadn't told the police…they would have thought she was crazy.

"It's probably nothing," she said in a tone that completely undermined any attempt at trivializing what was to follow. "But I don't remember hearing any footsteps. When I wear heels to work, my steps echo in there for days, and he was wearing nice leather dress shoes polished to a shine. Even if they were soft soled, the floorboards creak at the slight shift in weight. Bu I didn't hear him enter or leave the chapel. I thought I mus have misremembered or not been paying attention because it just doesn't make sense otherwise." Zoe turned to her new confident and asked wide-eyed, "Do you think I should have told someone?"

"You're telling me," he pointed out and her transient anxiety melted away. "What did you do after he left?"

"I radioed Eva to let her know he was coming. She asked if she could get the mother of the bride out of her hair, and I said I was almost done," Zoe paraphrased.

"How did Eva sound?"

"Fine. Well, she was about to throttle the mother of the bride, but that's normal," Zoe explained. "Weddings can bring out the worst in people and it was Eva's job to roll with the punches. That's why I deal with numbers. People stress me out."

"What happened next?" Morris gently led her further down the narrative.

"After a few minutes, I tried the walkie-talkie to let her know the wedding party could start decorating. She replied, but I couldn't make out what she was saying through the static. I asked her to repeat what she'd just said, but instead of Eva, I heard music followed by screams. That's when I hightailed it out of the chapel and followed the music to the Stutes Building."

Martinez observed Zoe as she spoke. She was speaking authentically, using words and phrases that would normally come out of her mouth, but the methodical order and her unnatural calm led Martinez to think she was in a suggestible state, not unlike hypnosis.

"And when you arrived?" Morris continued.

"The song ended and I opened the door. Everything a mess but no one was there. That's when I called 911."

"What can you tell me about the music?" he probed.

"It was an old Cajun standard called *Pa Janvier*, about a love-sick man asking for his sweetheart," she replied.

"Asking her father?" he guessed from the name.

"More like old man winter," she corrected his translation. "The young lady in question drove her carriage off a bridge and into the bayou after one too many drinks. You don't get more Cajun than that," she joked.

"That's an odd choice for music for a wedding," he remarked.

"It's very popular among musicians. Anyone that wants bayou cred performs it and you can't get through a Cajun music festival without hearing it," she laid out the facts for him.

He felt another tug. "How did this rendition strike you?"

Zoe turned quiet and looked off in the distance, searching for the right words. "I'm no musician and Cajun love songs never end happy, but there was something so utterly wretched about it. You could feel it in your soul." She instinctually reached for her locket, feeling soothed at its presence. Even though it hung under her shirt, Morris could see the charm for what it was.

She shifted her gaze to him. "Can I ask you something?"

"Of course, but I may not have the answer," he prefaced.

"Why those women instead of me? He saw me first. I was alone. It would have been so much simpler…" her voice trailed off without finishing the sentence.

Morris felt the raw nerve buried under all the protective layers and modulated the shape of his will, coating it with balm. "I've seen a lot of terrible things in my line of work and try as I might to understand why they came to pass, it isn't always possible to know. When that happens, I stop asking why and focus on how to move forward with what I have been given."

His voice was the vocal equivalent of a warm glass of milk and a toasty blanket. Even Martinez felt a tingle in her toes, and she was not the target of his will. "Nothing can change the past, and if someone has their hand on you, it would be a waste of a boon asking questions to which there are no answers."

Martinez felt someone approaching the door and signaled to Morris by clearing her throat. He carefully withdrew his will the same way as he'd entered, gradually reintroducing distance in the intimacy he'd created. Zoe's breathing returned to normal and she blinked a few times, slightly disoriented but noticeably calmer. The crisp knock at the door severed any lingering connection she'd had to Morris as she fully came to.

She walked to the door and cautiously called out instead of opening it right away, "Who is it?"

"Wok and Roll. Delivery for a Z. Miller," a muffled voice yelled from outside the door.

"Just a minute," she hollered back, before addressing her two unwanted guests. "That's my dinner. Are we done here?" The sass in her delivery let Martinez know Morris was done— Zoe was back in full form.

They rose from the couch and Martinez extended her card. "Thank you for your time, Ms. Miller. You've been very helpful. If you think of anything else, feel free to call this number."

Chapter Eleven

Martinez took a long satisfying swig of her cold beer and watched the lime wedge bob in the bottle as she set it back down on the table. Despite its leisurely start, it had been a busy day. Local law enforcement rarely welcomed federal involvement, but it was necessary for them to perform the procedural song and dance in case either she or Morris had left any trace DNA in the chapel.

She was confident they wouldn't find their fingerprints, but she couldn't be sure there wasn't a rogue hair or random skin cell shed in the crazy wind of the ritual. Sloppy collection and processing of evidence was an easy sell as long as they gave them a plausible scenario.

She helped herself to more chips and salsa and scanned the room one more time. Happy hour ended thirty minutes ago, but the bar was still packed with people celebrating the end of the workweek with copious amounts of alcohol. The restaurant was slowly filling up but a few empty tables remained. In the center of the dining room was one long table made by shoving multiple tables together. Based on the number of high chairs the staff had pulled out in anticipation of the large party, Martinez hoped her food would arrive shortly.

Morris had been quiet on the drive over. Except for basic pleasantries and ordering, he hadn't said much since they left Miller's apartment. He was obviously chewing on the case. Every so often, he made little grumbles and curious facial expressions as he thought things through and argued all sides.

While Martinez generally respected people's processes, patience was not one of her strong points, and it only got worse when she was bored. "Penny for your thoughts?" she broke the silence.

"What?" Morris uttered when it finally registered that he was being addressed.

She pointed her beer at him. "You're cooking up a theory. I can smell it. I know you are used to working alone, but you've got a perfectly good sounding board sitting right in front of you. So out with it."

Morris grinned at her pluck but hid it behind his rum and coke. "I think our spirit is an Acadian looking for his woman, who may or may not be named Pauline. My best guess is that they were separated in the Grand Dérangement."

"Was that so hard?" Martinez asked him facetiously, glossing over the fact that she no idea what the Grand Dérangement was. "Okay, so we give that to the analysts and see if they can find a connection. Maybe we can locate the woman before the poltergeist does, and you put him to rest before he can do any more damage."

Morris shook his head. "The woman is most certainly dead. The Grand Dérangement happened over 250 years ago."

"Oh," was all she could think to say.

Morris gave her a scornful look. "You visited the Acadian Village yesterday. Didn't you see something about it? It's pretty much the defining event to the Acadians."

Martinez squirmed in her seat as she bought some time with another sip of beer. She had never been called out for being unprepared. "I went there and hit the places of interest as it pertained to the missing women and left," she replied. Her explanation didn't wipe the judgy look from Morris's face.

"In my defense, it seemed more important to obtain an exclusionary salting of the sole witness to a supernatural being—one that ended up being a poltergeist on steroids, I might add—than wandering a fake bayou and reading plaques. And there was nothing at the time to suggest Acadians would play a significant role in the investigation," she argued.

Morris softened his demeanor and gave her a pass, recognizing that he'd hit some sort of nerve. "Okay, that's fair." He straightened up and puffed out his chest. "Time for a quick history lesson. Listen up because I'm about to school you on Acadians."

Martinez pushed the chips and salsa to the side and leaned in. She'd never seen professorial Deacon before. "Lay it on me."

"The Acadians were French settlers that landed in Nova Scotia in the 1600s, well before Jamestown. Things were bad for them in Europe between religious wars, disease, famine, and generally being poor, but they had one thing going for them: they were farmers who knew how to work with crap land. They made friendly with the local Indians—"

"First Nations," Martinez interjected.

"The Mi'kmaq," he one-upped her. "And in a spirit of cooperation, they built a nice life for themselves in the New World and grew rich from agriculture, fishing, hunting, crafts, and trade as more Europeans crossed the Atlantic.

"England and France were at war with each other all the time, and that spilled over to the New World. The Acadian real estate flip-flopped between British and French a dozen times, but there's two things you need to know about the Acadians.

"First, the Acadians still thought of themselves as French, even though they had spent over a century in the New World. They spoke French, and their food and music was still very French. Second"—he counted on his fingers—"they didn't care who was in charge as long as they could do their thing. British, French…it didn't matter who officially ruled as long as they were left alone to prosper and trade. For a long time, the powers that be tolerated it because they were so far from home and needed the goods and services the Acadians provided.

"All that changed when the British came out as the definitive victors. They wanted the Acadians to swear unconditional allegiance to Britain and sign an oath. To the Acadians, that was nonsense—they were there before the British and minding their own business. In their minds, they didn't have to sign shit. So the Acadians strung them along without actually signing because once they signed, that was all the British would need to confiscate their possessions and punish them for trading or helping the French or any of their allies.

"When the French and Indian War broke out in the middle of the 1700s, the British came down hard, demanding the Acadians promise not to help the French. But the Acadians were proud and still considered themselves French. Even if they were tempted to sign just to shut the British up and continue doing what they liked on the down low, they certainly weren't going to do that now, just to spite the British. So the British took their stuff anyway, burned down their communities, and kicked the Acadians off the land they had worked for over a hundred years."

Morris spread his hands out with a flourish. "That is Le Grand Dérangement."

"That's terrible, but I suppose Americans picked it up from someone…" Martinez snidely remarked. "What happened to the Acadians?"

"Some were shipped to one of their North American colonies, other were deported back to France. The point was to break up the Acadian community so they wouldn't be a threat to British interests, but in reality, families were separated and a lot of Acadians died in the relocation. Not all the ships made it to their destinations," he added gravely.

A light came on in Martinez's brain. "Maine, Connecticut, New York, Virginia—they're all originally British colonies," she said, nodding. "But where does Louisiana come in?"

"The survivors regrouped afterward and some returned to the northeast, but a contingency went to Louisiana in the second half of the 1700s. They wanted to get away from British control and Louisiana was owned by Spain at the time, who was too busy trying to keep its empire together to pay attention to some French-speaking refugees living in the bayou. By happenstance, it was briefly French when Spain lost it in a war, but France sold it to America shortly thereafter to pay off war debts."

Martinez dug deep in her memory for US history and had the Louisiana Purchase filed somewhere after Independence but before Manifest Destiny. Morris took advantage of the pause to grab a few chips from the basket and wash them down with a splash of rum and coke. All this talking woke up his appetite.

"So why are they Cajuns instead of Acadians?" she puzzled.

"Ah, now you are talking about race," Morris warned her before proceeding. As a black man, he'd learned to be delicate about such things and gave her time to change subjects. When she made no such gesture, he continued. "The Acadians in Louisiana were far from Nova Scotia and France. Time and isolation changed their language and culture into its own thing—a French base peppered with Native Americans, African slaves, and other European groups. Over time, Acadian was abbreviated to Cajun, the same way Indian became Injun. While some Cajuns embrace all those different influences, others want to align more closely to their French ancestry."

Martinez read between the lines and scoffed. "White people are the worst." Morris nodded but said nothing. Sitting in a packed Mexican restaurant on a Friday night, she was light enough to get away with saying that. He was not.

"Why do you say her name may or may not be Pauline?" she brought up another point that was unclear to her. She could tell by the look on his face that he felt particularly clever for working this one out.

"Communication with undead can be tricky," he began. "Even when you speak the same language, there is room for interpretation. Take, for example, when Zoe corrected me. Pa Janvier could be how someone addresses the male head of the Janvier household, though in true French it would be *Père* Janvier. But, like Zoe mentioned, it could also be translated as *Father January*, which English speakers would more commonly refer to as old man winter, a very distinct avatar of death. If our spirit is in Cajun country and trying to communicate the idea that he's desperately looking for his lost love, he might just play this song, especially if none of the women spoke French."

Martinez was getting used to his style of teaching, circling the topic before pinning it down. "Sure, like how some people on the internet reply to things with memes. They are communicating symbolically through shared metaphors."

He gave it some thought. He would have called posting only in gifs and with memes asinine, but her way sounded more academic. "Sure, something like that."

"Hard to believe speaking French saved Zoe's life. Score one for language teachers everywhere," she toasted before taking another sip of beer.

"Everyone wants to be understood and heard, which is hard to do if you don't speak the same language," he concurred. "But the charm she was wearing also helped. My guess is that it is some sort of family heirloom that one of her ancestors enchanted."

Just then, the kitchen door burst open and the waiter called out "hot plate" to warn the nearby waitstaff and guests as he made his way to their table. There was no smoke and sizzle—neither of them had ordered fajitas—but the smell was amazing nonetheless. She was suddenly very glad she didn't fill up on chips and salsa.

"I've got a chile relleno," the mitted waiter announced.

"For the gentleman," Martinez answered.

"Be careful, sir, that plate is hot," he warned Morris as he set it down with a stack of warm flour tortillas. "Which means you must be the tamales." He turned to Martinez and presented her with the other dish. "Bon appétit!"

While Morris started sawing into his deep fried cheese-stuffed peppers, Martinez simply stared at her plate. She was fine with the tamales being unwrapped, although she preferred to do that herself, but she couldn't understand why they were so small and smothered in red sauce and cheese. "What is this?" she asked, confused.

"You ordered tamales. That's how they do tamales here—delta style," he stated it as fact. Martinez pushed the food around with a fork, suspiciously examining it from all angles. She had heard of the variant before but had never eaten it. "Trust me, they're good," he reassured her. "Until this morning, you'd never had oysters for breakfast and look how well that turned out."

Martinez cut through the soft corn casing with her fork and took a bite. First impression, it was hot—like pica mucho, borderline pica demasiado. Tamales should have a spicy filling, but the masa itself should be kind of bland. That's what roasted jalapeños and salsa were for—to add as much heat as desired. As it slid across her tongue, the surface was completely smooth. The characteristic ridges from being cooked in cornhusks were nowhere to be found.

As she chewed, she noted the difference in texture. The corn was grainer than she was used to and less fluffy than it should have been. As for the filling, the shredded pork was juicy and flavorful, which was tasty, but still all wrong. All the moisture should have been absorbed into the corn paste when they steamed it.

As she mentally dissected her food, Morris watched her like she was the dinner entertainment. "What do you think?"

"It's good," she said weakly. "It's not tamales, but it's good." In the spirit of fairness, she took another bite.

"Do you want some of my relleno?" he offered.

"Yes, please," she said sweetly and carefully pushed her warm platter toward him. "I'll finish the one I've already started, but you can have as much of the rest as you want." Morris flagged the waiter down for extra plates and started moving food around.

The great tamale debacle opened the door for a conversation about cooking. He told her all about how delta-style tamales—aka hot tamales—came to be and the adjustments that were made to accommodate palette and available resources. It was a lot easier and cheaper to get cornmeal and parchment paper than lime-soaked masa and dried cornhusk in the deep south in the early twentieth century. When they couldn't afford meat, they spiced the corn mush and ate that, and the practice stuck in more prosperous times.

Morris attributed the spiciness to white people not seasoning their food enough. He hated to confirm a stereotype, but it was true—black folks need flavor. He had no explanation for boiling over steaming, except that it was less involved and only required a pot. Once the decision was made to season the corn meal and boil the tamales, if only made sense to cook them in something tasty which could be ladled over them as gravy.

Martinez told him all about the best tamales she had ever eaten: her grandmother's goat head tamales. Martinez had the recipe, but they never turned out quite right. Plus, getting her hands on a goat head was as difficult as one would imagine. She could still remember watching her abuela work, a one-woman tamale-making machine. Her hands moved with a speed that could only be obtained by muscle memory. For every one Martinez made, she'd have three on her side and be halfway through making the fourth.

It was nice to put work away for half an hour and be social over shared food. While she declined a second beer, she didn't object to Morris getting another rum and coke. However, she couldn't say no to a flan, especially after skipping over the pie case at breakfast. There was only so much willpower she could muster on the road.

Martinez carved into the creamy custard with her spoon and savored the milky caramel goodness. This was definitely flan. She didn't speak until it was finished.

"You know what I'm thinking?" she said as she put her spoon down.

"Order a flan to go for later and park it in the hotel mini fridge next to the chicken?" he teased her.

She gave him a dirty look. "No. I'm wondering what makes a spirit wait centuries before suddenly going full-on poltergeist."

"How much do you know about poltergeists?" he asked.

"Just what I read in the twins' primer," she admitted.

"Then you know the basics," he translated for her. "Undead are dead things that exist in the mortal realm, but dead things belong in the land of the dead. In order to make and maintain a connection to the mortal realm, they need power. That's why so many corporeal undead kill things—they take the raw energy from the living and use it as fuel."

"So zombies don't really crave brains?" she wryly asked.

He gave her a stern look. "Are you going to take this seriously?"

She pulled herself together. "Yes. Sorry. The flan is going to my head. Please continue."

"For undead without a body, they have to find other ways to muster energy. That's why people often perceive cold spots before a spirit manifests—it's using the heat in the air as fuel," he explained. "The nastier ones have figured out how to kill people without physically harming them, things like banshees, specters, and dullahan, better known as headless horsemen."

"Headless horsemen? Like Sleepy Hollow headless horsemen?" she asked incredulously.

"Yep, they're real, although very rare."

"But poltergeists are different, right? They can touch people in the mortal realm even though they are incorporeal," Martinez anticipated his next point.

Morris nodded approvingly—she was paying attention.

"Exactly. It's quite clever when you think about it. They don't have to expend all that energy to maintain a physical body, but they can interact with objects and people when they want."

"But knocking a pencil off a table is orders of magnitude easier than stripping the flesh off a person," she pointed out. "Where is it getting all that energy?"

"That's where will comes in. You ever seen a hurricane?"

"Not in person, but I got close to a tornado working a case in Kansas," she answered.

"Same principle," he asserted. "When a poltergeist is triggered—and sometimes it doesn't take much—it can work itself up into a tizzy. If it holds on tight to all its anger, pain, and frustration, it creates a circular motion that can become a vortex, sucking in all the nearby energy." Martinez nodded. It jived with what she'd read; once a poltergeists becomes active, they escalate.

"So our spirit could have been chillin' in the land of the dead for ages before something triggered him, causing him to make a connection with the mortal realm and going full-on 'They're Here'?" she extrapolated.

"Exactly. Usually, it's not hard to find them and talk to them—figure out what triggered them and use that to disrupt and disperse that energy. That effectively severs their connection to the mortal realm. But there's not much I can do if I can't find the sonofabitch," he muttered. It was the first derisive reference she'd heard him use against the poltergeist since he'd arrived in

Lafayette.

"Can we summon him and jump him?" she spitballed. Her first summoning was a ghost. Granted, it was her housemates who were even nicer than Casper.

"Not a bad thought, but we don't have enough on him to do it safely," he dismissed the suggestion.

"He speaks Cajun music. Can we lure him out Pied Piper-style and neutralize him?" she proposed. A practitioner could lace music with magic just as easily as words.

The half a minute Morris gave this idea told her it had legs. "Possibly. I can do the ritual by force, but it's significantly harder and it's messy. That's why I try to persuade them instead. Restless spirits are like pigs—you can lead them anywhere with a slop bucket, but they will dig in as soon as you try to push them from behind."

A spark went off in Martinez's brain. "What if we could get you more information…would that make it easier to talk him down?"

"Sure, but we don't have much to go on. I suppose the analysts might find something with the Acadian angle, but we are talking about events that happened before the US was even a country. And last I checked, we're all out of witnesses."

"Human witness," she pointed out.

He didn't like the glint in her eye. "I don't deal with devils," he said flatly.

"I don't blame you," she agreed wholeheartedly, "but I was

thinking of the guides."

The guides were three sisters that liked to voyeuristically watch the mortal realm from their native plane. They prided themselves on being fair and neutral parties in the greater supernatural world and could show a practitioner many things, if they were so inclined. They were favored by diviners and those that scried because their price for knowledge was low compared to other beings one could summoned for information. However, they always retained the right to refuse service. The nice thing about the guides was that they had a different sense of time.

"If anyone witnessed what happened to this guy, it would be them," she argued.

Morris mulled it over and reluctantly agreed. "They might help. They are suckers for a tragic love story. How's your relationship with them?"

Martinez wobbled her head equivocally. She'd had a rough start; the guides only cooperated when all three reached a consensus, which could be tricky. But once she figured out that mortals were their reality TV, she learned how to adjust her sales pitch. "They haven't turned me down in a while, but I don't ask lightly," she answered honestly.

When the subtext of the question sunk in, Martinez turned the tables. "Wait, why do you need me to do it? I saw you with Zoe. You could charm the scales off a fish."

"It's complicated," he said with chagrin. "Let's just say I

learned the hard way that sisters talk and you shouldn't try to play one off the others."

She shook her head. "Oh, Deacon." She flagged down the waiter and asked for a flan to go and the check. Morris said nothing but didn't try to hide the smirk on his face. She shrugged, "It was a good idea and summoning makes me hungry," she said in a low voice once the waiter was safely out of earshot. "Now, what do we need to pull this off?"

Chapter Twelve

In the world of summoning, the guides didn't require much in terms of material components, but a practitioner had to have these basics. First: chalk to make the circle because nothing was truly safe when a practitioner makes a connection to another plane. Second: candles, convention dictated scented. As far as Martinez could tell, the actual scent didn't matter as long as it fully engaged the sense. She wasn't much for scented candles normally, but she tried to pick something she found nice so she could use it to immerse herself in the ritual.

Third, a reflective surface. The guides were able to speak to those that sought information, but they preferred to show rather than tell—a picture's worth a thousand words. Dedicated scriers had a favored mirror or crystal ball, but any reflective surface would work. In the past, Martinez once made do with bottled water poured into the largest Pyrex pan she had in her kitchen.

On paper, summoning the guides on the road should have been a piece of cake. Chalk, both white and blue, was standard travel gear in her suitcase. Scented candles were ubiquitous, sold in every home goods store, craft store, and most grocery stores. Hotel bathrooms were covered in reflective surfaces.

The problem came in engineering a setup where Morris could observe remotely because of the bad blood between him and the sisters. Thankfully, they were living in the age of video calls. While Martinez summoned them in the bathroom, Morris could be out of sight but watching.

Martinez preferred to put the reflective surface in the circle to keep their magic bound, but that wasn't possible in this bathroom. The large mirror above the countertop was bolted to the wall, and the full-length mirror hanging behind the door was too long to circle. She could circle the sink, but it didn't have a great stopper and she worried it wouldn't hold enough water to last the entire time. It wasn't like she could top off from the tap mid-summoning. There wasn't enough clearance in back to circle the toilet, but this was no great loss as far as Martinez was concerned—scrying out of a commode felt categorically wrong. The only time she wanted to be on her knees in front of the john was if she needed to puke, and even then, it wasn't really a question of want.

After long consideration, the bathtub ended up being the best of a slew of suboptimal choices. She still couldn't put a hollow circle around it, but at least it provided a large viewing area and held plenty of water to last through the whole summoning.

The drain was sealed and the cold water going full throttle—she wasn't getting in and the last thing she needed was steam. She pulled the shower curtain to one side and secured it before jerry rigging a stand for her phone out of standard hotel kit. She engaged the speakerphone and positioned her phone on the counter.

"How's that angle?" she checked in with Morris.

"I can see the water," Morris replied.

Martinez knelt in front of the tub. "Am I blocking your view?"

"No, I'm good," his full voice sounded from her phone's speaker, but she could also hear him through the door. He wanted to be close by in case things went pear-shaped. "You really think this is going to work? It's not too late to scrap this idea, get a bowl from the hotel kitchen, and do it together. At least I could help power the summoning, and they'd be in the circle," he reasoned.

Three months ago, Martinez would have wholeheartedly agreed with him. Her first ride along with Wilson boiled down to a summoning-gone-wrong, and she could gladly go her whole life without having a fiend know the taste of her blood. But summoning wasn't just about demons and devils, and her experience in the Upper Peninsula showed her a way to communicate with helpful supernatural beings without protective circles. Not that she was ready to forgo the chalk altogether, but she was willing to try contacting the guides in this manner.

"I appreciate your concern, but they like me, remember? It's you they got beef with. You'll be watching and listening the whole time and if things look dicey, you're right on the other side of the door," Martinez reassured him.

He harrumphed. "For the record, I don't like it."

"Your objection has been noted," she replied as she continued getting the room ready.

In case of catastrophic failure, she closed the lid on the toilet and padded the floor with a towel. There was never a good time to wreck your phone, but in the field was the worst. She tore open the packaging on the candles—a six-pack of gingerbread votives found in the discount bin of the drugstore down the street. The room filled with the smell of cinnamon, nutmeg, and ginger.

She turned off the water and lined the edge with used towels to prevent any splashed water from going very far. The tub was only half-full, but the waters could get turbulent and she'd never had the guides outside of a circle before. She grabbed a full salt canister and popped the metal sprout, pouring a continuous ring around the rim of the tub. It wasn't as good as a proper hollow circle, but it was a boundary of sorts, more akin to privacy fence with a *no solicitation* sign on the door instead of an electrified fence labeled *trespassers will be shot*. She lit and placed five candles within the salt so the guides could find the water, like lighting up a runway for airplanes landing at night.

With the bathtub staged, she stepped back and slipped off her clothes. The last few times she'd been successful, she was naked as a jaybird, and Martinez wasn't one to fix what wasn't broken. She caught her movements in the chrome fixtures and the shower wall, but there wasn't enough detail to cause her any concern. Deacon liked the ladies, but he didn't strike her as a creeper.

She made a cushy square for her knees by folding a towel twice over and knelt on the floor. Everything she needed for the ritual was beside her: chalk, a candle, a lighter, her rosary, and a sample of the wax and wick from Deacon's ritual candle.

With the chalk, she marked her circle on the white tile, closing herself in until the ritual was finished. If she couldn't put the reflective surface in a circle for protection, she would put herself inside one. She carefully formed each sigil, attaching it back to the circle just so. She used blue chalk to make sure the seams of grout were adequately covered, something she never had to worry about on the single slab of slate in the concealed ritual room in her Corktown basement. A protective circle was no good if it was broken.

When she was satisfied with her work, she called out to Morris. "Are you ready?"

"Radio silence starting now," he replied before hitting mute and covering his camera.

Martinez lit the last candle and cleared her mind. As the

warm spices filled her nostrils and entered her body, she stilled herself. Rosary in hand, she said a Hail Mary to focus her will.

"I beckon the sisters three, whose noble hearts are not unmoved by injustice and tragedy. Alia, young and fair whose mercy knows no limit. Moirae, dark and inscrutable whose vision knows no bounds. Sarce, matronly and wise, whose judgment knows no equal. Bless this humble mortal with your presence and grant her audience to make her plea."

Martinez waited, will extended. She knew to proceed when the flame of her candles flickered and a gray mist filled the still water. "To the guides that watch over us, I ask for your guidance. A wretched spirit roams here, taking life without regard. I beseech you to show me what binds this tortured soul to the land of the living so that I may help him find peace."

Martinez held the white wax shavings and burnt wick above her candle. "Smell his heinous works and know the torment behind them." She dropped them in and let it burn in her fire. The water in the tub bubbled from below, agitated by the acrid smell of the poltergeist's deeds.

She closed her eyes and lowered her forehead to the cold tile. The entreaty was made and there was nothing more to do but wait for the guide's decision. Prostrate and laid bare before them, she repeated the same words in supplication, winding her will around each syllable. "Hear my plea."

The guides, who had seen all that happens in the present, past, and future, had much to consider. Her request was honorable but it was tainted by association. It was two versus one, but Moirae's objection was not so vehement to warrant outright refusal. Instead, she gave the petitioner a chance to explain herself.

The water bubbled and a voice crossed the veil. "Do you ask this for yourself or for another?"

Shit, Morris thought and readied himself to bust through the door if necessary.

Martinez kept her heart pure and answered honestly—you couldn't fake authenticity with the guides. "It is true that I work with another, one that has offended your esteemed persons, but I would never insult you with his presence. I am before you, and it is not on his behalf that I act.

"I call upon you on behalf of Eva Chapman's children, so that no one else has their mother taken from them too soon. I call upon you on behalf of Eileen Parker, so that no other parent is robbed of walking their child down the aisle. I call upon you on behalf of Ashley Downer and Mabel Kies, because sisterhood should not end in such dishonor. I call upon you on behalf of Kaylee Parker and Leland Kirkwood, two souls now separated by death whose love was cut short. I beg of you, for them, hear my plea."

Oh, she's good, Morris said to himself as he heard her supplication through the door. He watched on his phone, waiting to see how the guides reacted.

Martinez kept her head down and continued her litany.

As long as the water was moving, it meant they were still considering her petition. The answer may not yet be yes, but it wasn't no either. It must have been a spirited debate because the water was churning.

Alia pleaded for compassion—wasn't that soul long overdue for some peace? Sarce made a case for minimizing future suffering—misery begat more misery. Moirae saw the rightness in her sisters' words, but was most moved by the petitioner's integrity. Even when exposed, she spoke the whole truth.

When Moirae joined her sisters, a consensus was reached and they spoke as one voice. "Raise your eyes and see what the waters have to show."

Martinez obeyed and peered into the bathtub as the gray haze parted. It was a wedding—not in the New Hope Chapel, but not one so different from it, either. It was whitewashed and bright with exposed beams, and standing at the simple altar was a couple taking vows to God and each other.

The groom was immediately recognized by both agents. He was younger and certainly happier than in the Lafayette PD's sketch of him, but there was no doubt it was the same face—the aquiline nose, the high cheekbones, the thin lips, the square jaw, and those intense brown eyes. Beside him stood a dark-eyed beauty with auburn hair. She wore a cornflower blue dress trimmed with lace, and her hair was braided with yellow ribbons and small white flowers tucked into the folds. He beamed as she placed a plain ring on his finger.

The surface rippled as that scene faded and another began. Now, he was in a workshop with tools hanging on the walls and sawdust on the floor. Perched on a horse bench of his own making, he was attaching spindles to a frame with delicate precision. His strong, dexterous hands were rough and calloused, and the iron band was still on his finger, although speckled from sanding wood with fine grit. He ceased his work and wiped his hands on a rag when his wife entered the workshop to see his progress. He turned it over and she ran her hands across the proto-crib. Her swollen belly poked ever so slightly under her dress, which he touched in an unguarded moment of tenderness.

Martinez's heart skipped a beat as a stream of water shot straight up and fell back down, breaking over the image of a baby's brow. The bathroom filled with its cries as the water slicked back its dark curly locks. It shivered at the cold water as the priest gave a benediction and completed the baptism, claiming its soul for God. An anonymous hand made an addition to a long ledger of names and dates: Jean à Hugo, May 12, 1757. In the other room, Morris grabbed a pen and started writing it down in case the recording failed.

Then, the water became dark as did the mood. Even the bathroom lights seemed to dim. Points of light dotted the inky surface and Martinez could smell the smoke on the horizon. As the shot crested a ridge, she saw armed men on foot and horse, wielding guns. Women and children were fleeing their homes before the soldiers or fire took them. She could hear their screams and gunfire.

The water lightened to pale blue but turned choppy, and the whole bathroom heaved and swayed. Anchored by the circle, Martinez was calm and centered, like standing in the eye of a storm. The water licked the sides of the bathtub, but didn't extinguish the candles or compromise the salt.

A ship came into view, flags flying high on the mast. It was listing badly to starboard and the men on deck were bailing, returning the water back to the sea as fast as they could. Across the stern, the letters dipped below the waterline: Duke Wi. The view zoomed in to one man in the line, passing full buckets toward the ship's edge and empty ones below deck. Dirty, bearded, and bedraggled, it was hard to see his features, but Martinez knew those eyes.

It pulled in so tight that the bathtub was filled with those intense brown irises, so deep you could swim in them. She felt their pull but stayed in her circle. Even through the screen, Morris could feel the fear and despair. Those eyes knew they were never going to see their wife and child again.

When his lids finally closed, the perspective pulled out, and he was on his knees in prayer. His clothes were soaked and the water came up to his hips. He held a rosary tight in his hands and the ring hung loose on his gaunt finger. Martinez couldn't understand the words, but she heard his prayers.

As all the color and texture disappeared from the water, the guides spoke again. "The spirit you seek has done great wrong, but in his heart, he is still this man."

Martinez praised them by name for the gift of their insight, bowing deep at the hips three times. When she came up the final time, the gray haze was gone, and the bathroom felt empty, hollow, and without meaning. With the link severed, she broke radio silence. "Did you get all that?"

"Yes. Are you okay?" She heard him in stereo—once through the phone and again through the door.

"Yeah, I just need a minute," she shakily replied. In previous encounters, the visions were flat, but these had a three dimensionality to them, and it wasn't just the theatrics. The guides had taken her on an emotional roller coaster. The adrenaline was still coursing through her veins.

"It was a wild ride," she explained. Her voice sounded steadier, and Morris relaxed a little on his side of the bathroom door. She pushed up on her knees and ended the video call with a tap on the screen.

"Don't take too long. You'll catch your death," he fussed like a mother hen. Part of him wouldn't believe she was all right until he laid eyes on her. To summon in one's birthday suit and without putting a circle around the summoning pool sounded crazy to him, but he also knew people thought the same about half the things he did.

"Why don't you send what we have to the Mine? I'll be right out," she suggested as she put on her underwear. She heard his steps move away from the door and finished getting dressed in peace.

She blew out the candles and put everything on the counter. Once the floor was clear, she wet a towel and mopped up the blue chalk, obliterating the circle and all the sigils. Then she used the same towel to sweep the salt into the bathtub and pulled the plug. In a matter of seconds, the water began to swirl down the drain, pressed by its own mass to obey gravity in the path of least resistance.

When she opened the bathroom door, she found Morris sitting in the high-backed chair next to the couch, elbows propped up on the armrest and thumbs tapping away on his phone. He had the biggest mobile she'd ever seen, and it was still too small for his large hands, as evidenced by how often he cursed under his breath when he hit the wrong letter.

She smiled when she saw her flan was already waiting for her on the coffee table, plastic spoon on top. She put her phone and rosary down and dove onto the sofa and into her flan.

"And sent!" Morris said victoriously. When he looked up from his phone, she was half-finished with her second dessert.

"Don't judge me. The guides are exhausting," she said between bites. The sugar rush was kicking in just as the adrenaline was wearing off.

He said nothing and lightly passed his gaze over her. She was tired, but okay. "I gotta ask. Why naked?"

"They kept turning me down and I really needed intel for a

case. When I asked Chloe and Dot for help, it was one of their suggestions. Apparently, I was 'too closed off.'" She vocalized the air quotes because she wasn't putting down her flan for anything.

"Well, whatever you did, it worked like a charm. Hopefully, the analysts will be able to pull something from this," he said optimistically.

"Could you hear them speak? I've always wondered if they were talking out loud or in my head," she asked as she took another bite.

"I could hear them, but that could be because they allowed it. Thought you were done for when they asked about me," he admitted. "But you did good."

Martinez accepted the compliment with aplomb. "What do you make of what they said at the end—that he's still that man?"

He sat back in the chair and assumed a posture of contemplation. "I would interpret that as a call for redemption."

She put down the now empty plastic clamshell and looked dubiously at him. "But he's a poltergeist with an anti-soul that's killed eleven people. And those are just the ones that we know of. How can anyone come back from that?" she asked skeptically.

"Grace," he replied simply. "Anyone can stumble into a pit of despair, but there is always a way out, no matter how far down they've fallen."

Chapter Thirteen

Lafayette, Louisiana, USA
1st of February, 6:00 a.m. (GMT-6)

The alarm went off at six sharp, and this morning Martinez heeded its call. The first thing she did was check her phone for a message from the Salt Mine. The analysts worked around the clock and it had been hours since Morris had requested a dig. She blew raspberries at her mobile when there was nothing new from them.

That was the way it was in the field—spurts of action with lots of waiting in between. It took a certain temperament to go 110% one moment, and null the next. However, she was well acquainted with the ebb and flow. It was yet another situation where her time in the FBI unwittingly trained her for the Salt Mine.

Martinez had honed strategy over the years to give her days order and direction while she was waiting for leads to pan out in the field. The key was incorporating flexibility into routine even though they seem diametrically opposed. She straddled the line by keeping busy doing productive things, but nothing that couldn't be dropped at a moment's notice when the case picked back up again.

If there was nothing new or pressing, she liked to start her day working out. Sometimes her accommodations had a gym, but it was just as easy to do calisthenics using body weight and things present in any hotel room—think Charles Atlas with more yoga. This morning, she put on her sneakers, popped in her earbuds, and went for a run. It had been months since she could run outdoors in fifty-degree weather, and she made room for serendipity in her routine.

It was still dark when she left, entirely too early and too cold for Louisianans to even consider exercise based on the look the night clerk gave her on the way out. They hadn't even set up breakfast or put out the complimentary newspapers. She decided to circle the long block because it gave her well-lit pavement lined with trees that avoided major intersections, even though there were few cars on the road at this early hour. It also meant she wouldn't be far from the hotel if her phone blew up with an update. She stretched out and found her stride.

After the first circuit, she picked up the pace; the path was known to her and she could anticipate patches of uneven pavement or curbs that suddenly dropped off. She found the steady rhythm of her breath and footfall therapeutic. She often went for a run when she was trying to clear her mind, work through some feelings, or solve a conundrum, but she had no such need at the moment. Today, she was just running for the joy of it.

When she returned, she headed to her room to do a long stretch and a quick shower. In case of a hasty departure, she draped her sweaty clothes over hangers to get them to dry faster before turning on the hot water. When she pulled back the curtain and stepped in, there were still grains of salt at the far end of the tub. She kicked warm water toward them to wash away the final traces of last night's summoning before soaping up and rinsing off. She dried off with the clean towels she had left and immediately checked her phone—still no word from the Salt Mine.

Martinez returned to her routine; after exercise and a shower, it was time for breakfast. She rubbed her hair vigorously before brushing it. She decided to go au natural and passed on the hair dryer and makeup. She pulled on jeans and a sweater because she had too much self-respect to roll into the dining area wearing pajamas. That was forgivable for children, petulant teenagers, sick people, and people that were coming in the last fifteen minutes of the breakfast, but grown-assed adults with time should know better.

The dining area had just opened for breakfast, and the first of the scrambled eggs, bacon strips, and home fries were under the heated lamp. There was a bank of toasters, and the breadbaskets were full of options. There was even a waffle maker—with cups of pre-measured batter—for the adventurous next to the cereals and the drinks station.

Martinez had stayed at the entire spectrum of lodgings in

her professional career—some of them real dives—and this was the cream of the crop as far as complimentary breakfasts go. Alas, after yesterday's food fare, none of it looked particular appetizing this morning. She grabbed herself a banana, a carton of yogurt, a box of corn flakes, and a hot cup of coffee with French Vanilla creamer before returning to her room.

Today's paper was waiting for her when she returned, and she tucked it under one arm as she made the same observation everyone does while standing in front of their hotel room: *I don't have enough hands to pull this off.* She juggled everything to one side and coaxed the key card in and out of the slot. Once inside, she dropped everything on the table. She kicked off her shoes and hit the mini fridge.

Cold fried chicken was the best leftovers for breakfast known to man. The only other food that came close was cold pizza. She fished out a thigh and bit down. The crust had lost much of its satisfying crunch, but it was still deep fried batter on chicken skin. Even when it wasn't great, it was good.

Had she been eating something less greasy and hands on, she would have taken this time to read the newspaper or reports on her phone. But since she was finger-licking deep in chicken fat, she decided to indulge in a little mindless TV. She found the remote and knuckled through the channels.

She skipped over the twenty-four-hour news stations, which were little more than a vehicle to dish out advertising, and it was too early for reality TV. That was "unwind at the end of the day with a glass of wine on the couch" sort of viewing. Then she hit kid's programming.

She was glad to see that Saturday morning cartoons were still a thing, but she didn't recognize many of the shows. When she tried the classic cartoons, they had been revamped for an entirely different generation. The characters basically looked the same, but the animation was different, the voices were slightly off, and the humor was more sophisticated than she remembered. When she found something that wasn't too manic, she sat back and giggled. It had been decades since she woke up early just to park herself in front of the TV, often with a bowl of cereal for breakfast.

She was halfway through her yogurt when her phone buzzed. She immediately contemplated if she could eat more in case it was Morris calling about breakfast out—maybe not the entire spread, but she was definitely good for a plate of fried oysters and another cup of coffee. She perked up when she saw three attachments from the Mine.

She sat up and switched off the TV. It was time to work. Crossed legged with her coffee close at hand, she scanned the brief message and opened the first attachment.

More than twelve thousand Acadians were expelled from Acadia between 1755 and 1764—seventy-five percent of their total number. In the summer of 1758, the British took Louisbourg and began the deportation of Acadians off Île Saint-Jean, now called Prince Edward Island. While the British had made previous attempts to resettle them in one of their thirteen colonies, they had largely abandoned the scheme to integrate the French-speaking Catholics into British colonial life. Instead, they decided to return them to France.

Nearly a thousand Acadians were loaded onto three ships in Louisbourg: *Violet*, *Ruby*, and *Duke William*. In October, they set sail in a convoy of nine but were separated from the other ships during a bad storm. They licked their wounds in the bay near Canso and left there in late November. Again, they ran into foul weather, and again they were separated.

Ruby crashed in the Azores, and 213 of the 310 Acadians aboard died. *Violet* sank at sea December 10, 1758. *Duke William* had *Violet* in their sights, but they'd sprung a leak themselves and couldn't come to their aid. All 280 Acadians loaded onto Violet drowned.

For three days, *Duke William* mounted a pump brigade, and it was all hands on deck, including the Acadians. The long boat and cutter were sent out to look for passing ships. While there was traffic, none stopped. On the third day, Captain Nichols abandoned the effort and the ship. He was not aboard *Duke William* when it sank twenty leagues from the coast of France on December 13, 1758 with 360 Acadians aboard.

"So much for the captain going down with his ship," Martinez muttered. She did the quick math in her head—that single attempt at expulsion killed 5% of the entire Acadian population in North America in deaths-at-sea alone.

One of the few Acadian survivors from *Duke William* was Jacques Girard, a priest on Île Saint-Jean that the captain took with him on the longboat. Father Girard carried with him the names of the dead, which he committed to record upon his return to North America. Among them was Hugo Dubois.

Martinez put two and two together. Jean à Hugo—John, son of Hugo. Finally, the man with the intense brown eyes had a name. Now she better understood the look in Hugo's eyes. Being close enough to see *Violet* go down but not being able to help. Bailing for three days, and seeing ships pass but never coming closer to help. Watching the captain and your priest save themselves while you died with the crew of your deporter. Succumbing to the cold vast blue somewhere between where your people came from and where they had made their home. What a terrible way to spend one's final days.

But what about his Pauline? Martinez wondered as she moved to the second attachment, which had a more substantial message. Usually, the analysts were brief and to the point, but they had a lot to say about the lack of Acadian genealogical records online and how frustrating searching them for usable information was. After a noble effort, they were unable to find records of Hugo's marriage to his auburn-haired bride, or the birth of their son.

However, in their quest, they stumbled upon the Acadian Research Center of Prince Edward Island, housed in the Acadian Museum. It was in possession of more than 4,000

Acadian family records—things like birth, marriage, and death dates—in addition to censuses and village parish records. Much was lost in the Grand Dérangement, and if those records existed, they would probably be there.

Martinez sipped her coffee and opened the second attachment. It was a series of articles pulled from the online archives of L'Acadie Nouvelle, a newspaper based out of New Brunswick owned by the largest French-speaking media company in the Atlantic. The analysts provided the original French content as well as an English translation.

The article series was equal parts puff piece and advertisement that chronicled the saga of returning Acadian artifacts from the wreck of *Duke William* to Prince Edward Island. For the past forty years, they had been housed in a dusty display in some provincial museum in Poitou, the western coastal region of France where many of the original Acadians hailed. After years of petitions and negotiations, they agreed to repatriate the items to the Acadian Museum for their permanent collection. As per the final article, they were now on display as part of a larger exhibit on the impact of Grand Dérangement on Île Saint-Jean. Martinez searched for the final article's date of original publication: November 20th of last year.

Before she could open the final attachment, Martinez got a DM from Morris. *U reading?* popped up in the dialogue screen.

Yeah. WTF Britain?! she typed back.

SM booking travel, he gave her a heads up.

France? she tapped out and included prayer hands.

Lol! he replied immediately. *PEI. Going in as IT.* Martinez wistfully sighed and said goodbye to the warm weather and sunshine. Prince Edward Island was one of the maritime provinces of Canada.

K dibs on window, she answered back before opening the last attachment. It was a primer on Acadian history and culture. She started reading while she waited for a travel itinerary. This time tomorrow, she would be Tracy Martin, plucky correspondent for the Institute of Tradition.

Chapter Fourteen

Geneviève Samson stomped the snow off her boots and wiped them across the mat while she fished out the key to the door. It was freezing and overcast, and the tall blue, white, and red flags in front of the building waved furiously and snapped in the wind. In other words, it was just another winter day in the maritime.

With three hundred years of history on the island, Acadian pride ran strong here, and the Evangeline region was its cultural heart on Prince Edward Island. People spoke French with an Acadian patois, and their side of Confederation Bridge bid everyone coming from New Brunswick "Bienvenue." Homes flew the Acadian flag: vertical blue, white, and red stripes with a gold star in the upper left hand corner. Village Musical Acadien kept the beat going all year round, and summer was one long kitchen party. It even held the honor of hosting the World Acadian Congress—a giant festival held every five years to celebrate all things Acadian.

The area was also home to the Acadian Museum, where

Geneviève was just coming into work. She still had fifteen minutes until opening—plenty of time to put her things away, turn on the lights, and open the front doors to the public. Not that she was expecting a rush. Peak season was summer. This time of year, it was the sort of attraction people went to when the weather prohibited winter sports. No doubt the latest batch of dry powder would call everyone to the slopes.

Which suited her just fine. The museum ran on a skeleton crew during the off-season, and if she wasn't needed up front, she could whittle away the hours in the library, officially called the Acadian Research Center. Before the British campaigns of expulsion, French Acadie centered on current day New Brunswick, Nova Scotia, and Prince Edward Island, and many families that settled elsewhere after deportation had their roots on the island. Thus, genealogy was a big draw for those tracing their ancestry.

All the records in the Research Center were donations, and family collections were often a cobbled mess, not unlike the kitchen drawer that holds all the manuals, extra screws, and unidentified parts that one dared not throw away. They knew to keep it, but not necessarily how to read it or take care of it.

A little more family knowledge slipped away with each handoff, and the only hope of preserving the knowledge of the past was rejoining them to the larger body of archives in hopes connections could be found. When a family did decide to turn over their treasured documents to the Research

Center, preservation was the first priority. Only after further deterioration was prevented did they try to put them in some semblance of order.

The Research Center was slowly digitizing records to make the information more readily available to researchers and genealogists, but there were major hurdles in the process. Taking high-resolution pictures and uploading them was easy enough, but completely unhelpful in a world that ran on databases and Boolean searches. That meant that documents had to be transcribed before they could be used in a meaningful way.

Transcribing for the Research Center was a labor of love, especially since there was no money to pay anyone to do it. The Prince Edward Island Museum and Heritage Foundation kept the museum lights on, and the money that was allocated to the Research Center went straight into preservation. The actual transcription was all volunteer based, and Geneviève contributed to the effort herself.

The primary difficulty was that everything had been written by hand up until very recently, and subsequently susceptible to transcription errors. In a cursive script, m, n, r, and u were often confused for one another, and no matter how careful one was to get it right in the present, it was all too easy for a past priest to have inadvertently changed the spelling of a name when he copied it from another church document recorded in a different person's handwriting. But that was just the tip of the iceberg, as Geneviève had learned over the years.

When the museum officially opened at one, she unlocked the doors and made sure the girl working the ticket counter was settled before heading to the library. She was anxious to continue the work on the large donation from the LaGroix family, and it wasn't something she could do in fits and starts.

It took deep concentration, because after she finished transcribing a document, she had to check it against other records to see if it shed light on something she'd previously done or perhaps linked with something else held in the archive. It was like doing a puzzle without a reference picture, and she knew full well that pieces were missing before she even started. Some would find it maddening, but as a seasoned genealogist, Geneviève found it an enjoyable challenge.

She was elbow deep in the past when a woman with long wavy brown hair entered the library and called out, "Hello? I'm looking for the Acadian Research Center."

"You've found it but it's not open to the general public," Geneviève curtly responded. She was pretty sure she had finally found Virgile LaGroix's father in the 1820 census before she had been interrupted.

Martinez traced the voice back to its speaker and cast her will long. "I'm Tracy Martin, correspondent for the Institute of Tradition. I'm writing an article on the Great Upheaval for our quarterly publication and was told you might be able to help given your experience with the genealogy records."

Geneviève's initial impulse to shoo away the interloper suddenly softened. Martinez's will poked and prodded, trying to find an in. "Martin," she said ponderously as it seeped into her subconscious. "There were Martins on Prince Edward Island before the expulsion. Do you have a familial connection here?"

Martinez had her hooked but she wanted to secure the line before reeling it in. "Maybe, I'm not sure. I recently found out that I have Acadian ancestry on my father's side and it's been a real learning experience. That's what prompted my interest in writing about Le Grand Dérangement. People just don't know the kind of persecution the Acadians went through."

Martinez's well-chosen words elicited the desired effect, and the genealogist nodded in complete agreement. "That's so true. Take a seat and tell me what you had in mind."

Martinez smiled and reinforced the connection. "I wanted to tell the story of forced deportation using a real family to show how devastating it was. With the press around the return of the Duke William artifacts, I found my way to Île Saint-Jean. I found a good candidate, but I couldn't find out more about his wife and child. Do you think you could help me?"

"I can certainly take a look," Geneviève answered. "What's the name?"

"Hugo Dubois. He died on *Duke William* and I know he was married and had a son named Jean before his death, but when I searched your archives, I could find anything, not even his wife's name," she spun her will with her tale.

Geneviève's mind thought about the heaps of old photos in the archives whose subjects' names had been forgotten. The best they could do was identify it with the donating family and give an approximate date based on the context clues in the picture. What she wouldn't do to give them back their names.

The older woman put the LaGroix documents back into the box and took off her gloves before going to the computer. "Can you spell that for me?"

"D-U-B-O-I-S."

She typed away at the keyboard. "Nothing in the years preceding the expulsion, but they make a reappearance in the 1830s. Let's try a different spelling," she suggested as she ran her fingers over the keys, including in the search as many creative spellings of Dubois as she could think of. "There was no standardized spelling back then and most people were illiterate," she explained. "I once had a Madam Baret recorded under three different spellings."

"That must make things complicated," Martinez observed.

The genealogist peered over her readers. "You have no idea." Her face lit up when her eyes returned to the screen. "We have something around the right time."

She opened on the earliest record in its own window. "A record of marriage between Hugo Debose and Simone Patry on March 13, 1756."

Martinez smiled—Pauline had a name. "That's amazing.

Any record of what happened to her after Hugo died?" she asked.

Geneviève plugged "Simone Patry" into the search engine. During colonial times, French law had women keep their family name from birth on official documents after marriage, including church records. It was undeniably helpful in tracing linage and making lateral connections because a woman's familial history wasn't lost or erased at the altar. However, married women often went by their husband's surname in the community, making it difficult to connect the women in informal records to the ones listed on marriage and baptismal certificates. It was rarely cut and dried in the world of genealogy.

"Looks like she returned to the island after the expulsion. I have a Simone Patry married to Edmond Debose in 1761," she replied.

"Any relation of Hugo's?" Martinez asked curiously.

Geneviève opened another window and did some cross-referencing. "His cousin," she said matter-of-factly before flipping back to the other screen. "I have a census that indicates they had seven children in the house, but I don't have birth records for all of them. And I have a record of her death in 1800."

"Was Jean one of the children living with them?" Martinez wondered.

"There is a Jean Debose but there is no way of knowing if that is the same one fathered by Hugo. Acadians were big on reusing Christian names, and if Jean was a family name, there would be more than one," Geneviève said authoritatively. Putting an Acadian family tree together was a lot like trying to keep track of who's who in a Gabriel García Márquez book.

"There is a death recorded in a village parish record for a Jean Du Bois in 1822. That would put him in his 60s, not impossible if he was long-lived. Or course, he could have died before Simone return to the island. He would have been very young during the deportation."

"Do you think I could have a copy of those so I could include them in the article?" Martinez requested politely.

The older woman smiled. "I can do you one better. I can email them to you. Where should I send them?"

*****

Morris ambled through the Acadian Museum at a leisurely pace, playing the part of interested tourist while he noted the entryways, checked the corners for cameras and motion sensors, and examined the display cases for signs of enhanced security. Their plan was to divide and conquer. Martinez would take the archivist while he looked for traces of the poltergeist.

The museum took their responsibility to preserve the items very seriously. The cases were climate controlled for temperature and relative humidity, and once he'd passed through the front foyer, there were no windows or bright lights in order to minimize ultraviolet light damage to the already aged items. The ambient light was dimmed with incandescent accents to draw the eye to displays and their informational placards in French and English. Incandescent bulbs may be passé with environmentalists, but they were inexpensive, readily available, and emitted very little UV light. It put the Acadian Village in Lafayette to shame, but it was par for the course in his estimation. Everything in Louisiana was slowly rotting and falling into the sea and they were sustained by it. In that way—and only that way—it was the Venice of the American south.

The permanent collection was organized chronologically, starting with the arrival of the first Acadians to the island in 1720 to the present. The items from *Duke William* were located in their own case between The French regime, 1720-1758 and The Restoration, 1758-1860, and that was where Martinez found him when she returned.

"Did you find anything?" she murmured. There were only a handful of people in the entire place and little risk of anyone overhearing them, but she had been conditioned to speak quietly in sacred spaces and extended the courtesy to museums and public libraries.

He pointed to the display case. "The ring, third item from the right." All the other surviving personal items were almost exclusively gold or silver, but this was iron—pitted and blackened, but intact.

"How the hell did it survive sitting in salt water for

centuries?" she marveled. She'd seen videos online of Coke eroding metal.

"My guess is that the spirit of Hugo Dubois was bound to the ring, and that very connection made it hardier than usual," he replied.

Martinez appraised the lock and the security under the guise of being really interested in the items within. After tonight, the Acadian Museum would be short one ring. "If the poltergeist was tied to the ring, why isn't he here?" she asked.

"That is a very good question. I've never known poltergeists to haunt items, but ghosts are sometimes tied to possessions that were significant to them in life. I suspect he wasn't always a poltergeist," he said prosaically.

Martinez frowned. "Even if he became a poltergeist on Prince Edward Island, that still doesn't explain how he ended up in southwest Louisiana."

"Correct. Something must have happened here. The timing is too coincidental. A month after this ring arrives in North America, the first set of bones appeared. But how did he get free of his tether?" Morris didn't even bother to hide his exasperation.

She had no answers but offered what she could. "If it helps, I hit pay dirt on Pauline."

He gave her a hopeful glance. "Do tell."

"Her name is Simone Patry. She returned to the island after the expulsion and remarried her late husband's cousin. They stayed here and had seven children, one of which may or may not have been Hugo's son, and she died at the ripe old age of 61," she reported.

"Keeping it in the family," he commented. "Any idea about what happened to the boy?"

"I hit a bit of a dead end there—no marriage records and he wasn't listed as the father on any baptism certificates. There was a death listed that could be within the expected lifespan of a man born in 1757, but it's impossible to know if that's Hugo's son. Alternately, the archivist said that he could have died before Simone returned to the island or moved away from the area as a young man. It's also possible he was here the whole time and the records have been lost over time," she relayed all she'd been told.

Martinez felt him feeding a nascent idea and quietly read the informational wall plaque while he schemed.

"We need to talk to someone in the know," he said resolutely when he finally spoke.

"What do you have in mind?"

He gestured around him. "This place is littered with personal items. I bet there are plenty of ghosts that could fill us in after dark."

Martinez raised an eyebrow and lowered her voice to a whisper. "Just to be clear, you want to hold a séance in the middle of a B&E." She had already accepted that breaking in was inevitable, but she didn't think they were going to stay around for a tea party.

He nodded his head in commiseration—he didn't like the idea any more than she did, but he needed to know what happened here. "You do know which side of the border we're on, right?" she subtly reminded him her FBI credentials meant jack squat in Canada.

"You've seen the security here…it'll be fine," he projected effortless confidence. "We've got the rest of the day to work out the details. In the meantime, there's a textile display I think you'll really like. Right this way, next to that door."

Chapter Fifteen

Miscouche, Prince Edward Island, Canada
2nd of February, 11:55 p.m. (GMT-4)

Ghosts were what was left after a person lost its body but its soul hadn't moved on. They resided in the land of the dead, but they could manifest in the mortal realm and visit their favorite haunts, usually at night and close to their own turf.

While some found the concept of the land of the dead disconcerting—a literal purgatory between life and some version of an eternal afterlife—others saw it as a place where the dead could have the verisimilitude of being alive without physical pain or ailments. They even formed little societies for protection; ghosts were an old method of powering enchanted items, and there was safety in numbers.

In undead terms, ghosts were a gray zone. They were not inherently evil and still had a soul, but they were not all benign either. Like humans, one had to allow for a wide spectrum of motivations, thoughts, and actions. Because they were dead, they had the potential for becoming the nasty sort of undead— the kind with a magical signature, an anti-soul, and a tendency to do harm—but most were perfectly content in their ethereal existence.

A practitioner could summon a ghost as long as they knew its name, but it was rather coercive, the spirit equivalent of grabbing someone off the street and shoving them in an unmarked van. The more genteel way of contacting them was a séance—an invitation that could be refused rather than a command that must be obeyed. Politeness aside, ghosts responded to séances because it allowed them to hitch a free ride into the mortal realm. Instead of having to power their own manifestation, they could use the practitioner's will.

Holding a séance didn't take a lot of specialized arcane knowledge. It was even possible, although unlikely, for a group of non-practitioners to successfully perform a séance, but it was exponentially harder without a magician to direct all that unfocused will.

Although rooted in a real phenomenon, the number of self-purported mediums was way off the mark, and the charlatans focused on the window dressing. If they couldn't produce a ghost, they could provide an experience. Attending séances became fashionable entertainment during the spiritualism craze of the nineteenth century, the pre-cinema equivalent of watching a scary movie. In the cultural consciousness, the theatrics became associated with speaking to ghosts even though they were not integral to the process.

Which was why Martinez was making a circle out of tea lights on the floor of the Acadian Museum. Neither was an arcane requirement for the séance, but ghosts had become fond of soft lighting and circles. It created a certain ambiance and everyone liked to be wooed, dead or alive. Will applied correctly was enough to open a channel, but the ghosts still had to be willing to talk.

Her reservations notwithstanding, everything had gone smoothly so far. The streets were dead and the door they rigged hadn't been touched. They'd managed to slip back into the Acadian Museum with no fuss—there wasn't much money left in the budget for a sophisticated security system after funding all the preservation. Plus, it seemed like a foolish way to spend it. It was hard for Canadians to imagine anyone stooping so low as to steal from the Acadian Museum—bless their heart.

Martinez had even gone so far as to pick the lock on the display case, but they left the ring inside. In light of the many points of incongruence Morris had run into on this case, both agents felt it unwise to make contact with Hugo's ring before they had more facts about how he became a poltergeist. It was one thing for a necromantic rookie like Martinez to not know what the hell was going on, but if something baffled Deacon, it was best to proceed with care. However, they did want to hold it in the same room as the ring—essentially asking a next-door neighbor if they had seen anything instead of the people two blocks down.

"I would have brought the gingerbread candles if I knew we were going to do a séance," Martinez drily remarked as she lit each of the white unscented candles in the perfect circle.

Morris smirked as he took out his silver cross from his leather bag. "No one likes a smart ass."

She caught his face in the flame of her lighter. "Then why are you smiling," she countered.

His grin deepened but he said nothing. Instead, he checked his watch. "Five minutes," he counted down.

"I'm done," she announced as she lit the final candle. He walked the perimeter and approved. The circle could be much smaller if one was performing a séance by themselves, but she'd made it four feet in diameter—small enough for them to cover the entire circumference between the two of them but large enough for ghosts to appear inside.

He fished out two small blister packs, each containing a pale green, diamond-shaped tablet covered in fine silver runes. Babel lozenges were a Weber original inspired by the telepathic communication of fae sigils, except these allowed the practitioner to verbally communicate with ghosts, even if they didn't speak the same language. After Weber fine-tuned the runes from the prototype, he improved the mouth feel and flavor—they were now available in spearmint.

"Remember what I told you," he coached Martinez as he handed her one. "No swallowing or chewing. Stick it under your tongue and let it melt. Follow my lead."

Martinez pulled out her rosary. "Got it."

They sat on opposite sides of the circle and popped the

tablets in their mouths one minute before midnight. The seconds ticked by and Morris waited until his watch hit 00:00—the witching hour. *I will fear no evil…*

He flung his will out and swung it in a circular motion, like a rope of pure energy. As it spun overhead, it created an arcane vortex. When it took a stable form, Martinez fed her will into the spout. *Hail Mary, full of grace…*

Without magical sight, the well of available arcane energy between them was imperceptible to those on the mortal realm. It was silent, invisible to the naked eye, and its twirl created no wind. Those sensitive to the esoteric might feel a slight charge in the air, like a build-up of static electricity right before a shock. But to any ghosts in the vicinity, it was a sensory feast as subtle as an inflatable noodle man on full blast with a blinking neon sign advertising "Free manifestations this way!"

Morris spoke in a melodious voice and modulated his pitch and cadence to the rhythm of his whirling will. With no proscribed incantations to get right, much of a séance was in the performance. "Spirits of the Acadia, I welcome you to my circle. One of yours is lost and I want to guide him home. Enter if your hearts are true and noble."

Martinez deemed it half-circus barker, half-evangelical preacher at a revival. Regardless how she felt about either tent-based event, he had an undeniable charisma. Within seconds, she could feel multiple pairs of eyes behind her, curiously peering from behind the walls and displays. It was one advantage of living with ghosts—she'd learn to recognize that change in the air when spirits were present.

The hair on the back of her neck and arms stood on end and her monkey mind was screaming alert calls, but her higher brain functions kept it in check. She didn't want to scare the ghosts off and they were right to be cautious. Some practitioners preyed on ghosts.

One of the candles between them flickered unnaturally, the first demonstrable sign that they weren't alone. Someone was in their circle. The air within the tea lights compressed as the spirit siphoned a little energy from the cyclone of will. A deep voice emerged out of nothingness. "Of which of our brethren do you speak?" Martinez knew it was French, but her brain automatically parsed it in English.

Morris knew they were being tested, as the spirit declined to fully manifest until it knew their intent. "Hugo Dubois, a man lost at sea in Le Grand Dérangement. He has come this way but since moved on, doing untold damage in his wake. I seek to know what happened here so that I may put his soul to rest." His voice resonated with righteous conviction.

The name caused a stir and the barometric pressure instantly bottomed out, causing Martinez's ears to pop. All the candles went crazy, flames akimbo.

Morris immediately adjusted his magic to soothe the rattled nerves. It was the first time Martinez had been in ritual with him, their magic intertwined. His suddenly tasted like

Red Vines and lemonade while reading comics in the shade on a sunny afternoon.

"I cannot end his misery without knowing what has passed. Please, speak to me the truth," he tried a different approach.

Martinez heard whispers all around her. They were discussing amongst themselves, but they were talking all at once. It was hard to make out a complete thought, even with the Babel lozenge, but she picked up snippets. *Impossible. Dangerous. Mad. Inconceivable. Ruinous.*

A pressure wave rippled out from the circle, silencing the chatter. Then a woman's voice spoke with poise, "If we tell you, you must promise not to bring him back to Île Saint-Jean." There was an iron strength behind the gentle voice.

"But he is a son of Acadia," Morris objected.

"That is our condition," she said firmly. Martinez heard pain and fear behind the resolve. And something else.

"Simone?" she wagered a guess.

The agents felt a pull on the vortex as more power was drawn off. A translucent woman emitting a soft glow manifested inside the circle. She was dressed in a simple frock with a shawl around her shoulders, and her feet didn't quite touch the ground. Her figure had plumped up and her vibrant auburn hair had faded to a dull brown with streaks of gray, but she still had those bewitching dark eyes and handsome features amidst the fine lines and wrinkles. "How did you know?" she addressed Martinez.

"Because only someone who once loved him would wish him well despite all the chaos his mere name elicits," she answered. The women locked eyes and understood each other, and Morris nodded for Martinez to take the wheel. "Please, tell us what happened."

Simone's shoulders relaxed and she began. "He was a broken man when he returned. He pined for vows that had long since ended with his death and could not accept that things had changed in his absence. And he never got on with his cousin," she added in that tone women only used with other women. "We tried to explain it to him, but he grew angrier and more belligerent when his expectations and demands went unfulfilled. We had no choice," she justified her actions without actually saying what had transpired.

"No choice to do what, Simone?" Martinez pressed gently.

"We cast him out," she confessed.

Martinez didn't know what that meant, but Morris did. The poltergeist didn't sever his connection to the place. They cut him loose and set him adrift, effectively banishing him from where he was meant to haunt. Simone couldn't have done this alone. It would have taken the entire local spirit community to pull that off.

"You have my word," Morris pledged once he understood the gravity of the situation. "I will not bring him back."

Relief flooded her ethereal face. "I told him our son had gone south, in hopes he would find solace there. I hope you find him and give him peace, but I know it cannot be here."

"We will do our best," he vowed. "We would like to take his ring? It may remind him of happier days and be a comfort to his battered soul." Martinez knew they were going to take it anyway, but she found his gesture thoughtful even if he wasn't technically asking permission.

"Take it," Simone quickly consented. "It only brings me sadness." Her form faded in front of their very eyes and tensions dissipated as word of the agreement spread through the community—Hugo Dubois would not be returning.

Morris slowed the spin of his will as he made his farewells. "Good Acadians, thank you for taking us into your confidence. Be well and go with God." As its velocity diminished, the whirlpool of their combined will collapsed. The séance was over.

Martinez started blowing out the candles closest to her. It would take time for the wax to cool and she was anxious to leave.

"Good call," Morris said from across the circle, extinguishing the candles nearest him.

"I had a hunch and went with it," she tersely replied. She could feel the room return to normal as the ghosts dispersed and went about their normal business. It was no fun watching the circus pack up and leave town.

From her backpack, she pulled out a 3 x 5-inch box that was three inches tall. Lined with lead and filled with salt, it was heavy for its weight, but the runes on the outside were another layer of containment. "Ready to get the ring?"

He pulled out his cross. "Let's do it." He opened the unlocked display case with his gloved hand and plucked the iron circle from its pillow. As soon as he made contact, the ring reflexively yanked on his soul. After centuries with Hugo, it had been left alone and unguarded.

Morris easily shrugged off its clumsy lunge but didn't see what was coming next. Rebuffed, the ring unburdened itself onto him. Like a rogue wave in the ocean, all the sorrows Hugo had shared with it—but now it shouldered alone—blindsided Morris. Two hundred years in the cold, dark sea with no one for company. Being brought to a land where French was spoken but still he was not understood—those shores were not his, even if they shared a language. Returning home to find nothing was as he'd left it. Losing his family again, this time in the land of the dead. And then, to be exiled. A man with no home. A person without a country. An outcast. A pariah.

Morris floundered in an ocean of sorrow, momentarily uncertain which way was up. He could hear the blood pumping in his ears and his grip around the large silver cross tightened. *I will fear no evil.* In the depths of the ring's despair, he heard a voice call out to him. "Deacon, can you hear me?" He swam through the anguish and followed it back to the surface. No matter how far down you fall, there is always a way back up.

He felt Martinez touch his arm and her face returned in his

vision after he blinked. Once he was making eye contact again, she adamantly spoke her will. "Clarence, let go of the ring." Her voice was like freshly fallen snow—stark and cold, but crisp and pure. It sliced through the misery and he loosened his viselike grip on the pitted iron. It dropped into the open box. His heart lightened as it sank into the salt under its own weight.

Martinez quickly closed and secured the lid before turning her attention back to Morris. His breathing evened out and his color returned, but she still felt the need to ask, "Are you okay? Do I need to take you to the hospital?"

He laughed so loud, it would wake the dead if the witching hour hadn't already been struck. "Don't worry, I'm not having a coronary," he reassured her.

She breathed a sigh of relief and cracked a smile. "Good. I'd hate to try and explain all this to an ER doc."

Chapter Sixteen

Charlottetown, Prince Edward Island, Canada
3rd of February, 06:05 a.m. (GMT-4)

Martinez lounged on the settee, sipping a cup of hot coffee as she looked out the window. The view from the penthouse suite was charming. The sun hadn't risen yet, but the moonlight highlighting the layers of clouds over the snowy streets and quaint buildings was something out of a painting.

Helms had booked them a last-minute special at a high-end hotel not far from the airport—his way of making amends for the twenty-six hours of travel they'd had on the way to Prince Edward Island. It was the kind of establishment that put its logo on everything, included the soft terrycloth robe she was currently wearing over her pajamas.

"I could get used to this," she called out to Morris, who was washing up before breakfast.

"It's the least he could do after those flights," he grumped as he exited the bedroom. Martinez had insisted he take the bed after what the ring put him through last night. "David would have never arranged such a nightmare."

He took a seat at the table room service had wheeled in

minutes earlier and poured himself a cup of coffee from the carafe. The romantic getaway special came with breakfast in bed for two, served on a starched white tablecloth with silverware tucked into folded cloth napkins. There was even a fresh flower in a small vase.

The spread was equally inviting. Martinez took the cover off her entree: a cheese omelet with rashers of thick cut bacon. She extended Helms some grace in light of the mini-feast. "Lafayette to Charlottetown isn't exactly a well-traveled route," she said before slicing a petal off the fleur-de-lis shaped pat of butter and smearing it across a warm roll. "And it wouldn't have mattered if we arrived a day earlier. The Acadian Museum was closed Saturday, although I would not have complained about staying two nights here."

Morris grumbled as he laid the linen napkin across his lap and changed the subject. "Any word from Chloe and Dot?" he asked as he cut into his own fluffy omelet.

"They said that as long as the ring isn't actually enchanted or cursed, a basic purifying circle made of baking soda should do the trick," she replied before trying the bacon—crispy but not burnt, just the way she liked it

"Excellent. We can set it up as soon as we get back and let it cook overnight," he said between bites. Their first flight was in a few hours—three stopovers over twelve hours, and they would be back in Lafayette armed with a much better idea of what they were dealing with.

"We've got to get rid of the bad mojo on that ring if we want to use it to bring in Mr. Dubois," he plotted out loud. His magic was based on empathy, and the first step was thinking about the undead as deceased people instead of monsters or objects. Calling them by their name was a good start at humanizing them.

"I find it weird that iron could absorb Hugo's trauma," she said as an aside. "Isn't it inert?"

"Chemically yes, but so is chalk and we use that all the time in rituals," he argued. "Iron's got good tensile and compressive strength, but it is susceptible to corrosion. Maybe the same is true for emotions. What are emotions but psychic energy?" he asked rhetorically and chomped down on a slice of bacon. His disposition was improving with a little caffeine and food.

"If it can absorb negative feelings, can we pre-load it with happy ones for Hugo?" she flipped the logic around as she dipped her knife into the tiny pot of strawberry jam.

"Possibly, if we had the luxury of time, but we've got to get to him before anyone else gets hurt," he said doggedly.

"Does this mean you've figured out how to pull this off?" she respectfully inquired.

"I've got the broad strokes, but I'm still working out the kinks. You can't expect a man to think on an empty stomach," he chided. "But one thing's for certain. We're gonna need a boatman and a fiddler."

*****

David LaSalle lived in a Craftsman bungalow in Brightmoor, a four-square-mile neighborhood along the northwest border of the city. Designed as a planned community for southern migrants drawn to work in Detroit's then-booming automobile industry, it was hit hard by the city's blight, so hard it picked up the nickname Blightmoor. The once-thriving working-class neighborhood became a ghost town of abandoned homes and shuttered businesses. Its parks and streets were riddled with the sort of crime that comes when people were out of work en masse, and those that were able to leave did.

When LaSalle moved into the neighborhood, housing prices and mortgage rates were both miserably low. He bought a house in the middle of the street for a song. Though he spent a lot of time at work, he never worried about his home or his possessions. It took one unfortunate break-in attempt for the rougher elements to realize there wasn't anyone in Brightmoor rougher than LaSalle. Even blighted, word traveled fast through the neighborhood. He became a fixture, a quiet hulk of a man at six-foot-three and 230 pounds. He kept to himself, but wouldn't tolerate anyone messing with him or his.

When the city came and razed hundreds of abandoned and damaged buildings, his street was not spared. Now his closest neighbors were the corner structures on either end of street, but he still purchased the empty lots on each side of his house in case the neighborhood filled up again. He valued his privacy, and it allowed him to have a sizable garage and garden next to his postage stamp lot.

Once he'd established his territory, he turned his attention to fixing the place up. Originally built in the 1920s as a low-cost, mass-produced single-family abode, the house itself was in shambles and in bad need of some TLC. Renovation was too mild of a term. He literally rebuilt it from the ground up.

He started with jacking the house and stabilizing the foundation. The interior was stripped to the studs and the layout redesigned to suit his purpose. He rewired the house, updated the box, and ran a line to the newly built garage. He installed a tank-less system and put in radiant heat when he redid the floors and bathrooms. All the old windows were replaced with triple-paned argon-filled modern varieties, and the century-old building was topped with a thick slate roof, giving it a gingerbread feel. He scoured antique stores, flea markets, and even the dump for fixtures and fittings to give the home history without compromising on efficiency, safety, or comfort. At the end of the day, he turned it into a picture-perfect, white-picket-fenced home with a garage-slash-workshop to one side and a raised-bed garden on the other.

He'd enjoyed working with his hands and the transformation was something he was proud of, but it was nearing the end. The necessary replacements and repairs had been done, and to do more would be gilding the proverbial lily. He was too practical to change things solely in the name of redecoration, and he wasn't sure what to do next. He supposed he could sell this place and do it all over again somewhere else. There was no end of rundown homes in Detroit, but he just got the house the way he liked it.

He was flipping through the seed catalogue trying to decide what to plant this year when his mobile rang. He rarely received personal calls, and it had been completely silent since he started his vacation. If it weren't for work, he would have foregone it altogether, but his job did not stop for nights and weekends. Agents in the field, Leader in the office, Chloe and Dot in the library, or Weber in his workshop—LaSalle was who they called when they needed something fast or direly.

"Hello?" he answered in his smooth tenor.

"David, it's me," Leader responded without identifying herself further because there was no need. "There's a situation."

LaSalle folded down the corner of the page to save his place and set it aside. Leader respected his time off, which meant whatever was happening was serious. "When do you need me to come in?"

"Deacon needs you in Lafayette, Louisiana. He and Lancer are already on route," she answered and gave him time to tease out the implications. Deacon meant undead. Lancer meant an investigation and probably a body with a possible FBI cover. Two agents meant the problem wasn't straightforward.

"Do I need to stop by the Mine first?" he asked.

"I've already got the sixth floor working on the package of requested supplies. All you'll need to do is pick it up on your way to the airport." LaSalle recalculated his route and added time in his head.

"Oh, and Deacon asked that you bring your violin," she passed along the unusual request. "I'm sending you what information we have." He knew Leader and the agents well enough to know what that was code for—light on details because Deacon's in charge and he was allergic to paperwork.

"Has my travel already been arranged?" he asked.

"No, I figured you'd rather do that yourself," she replied. Neither mentioned his temporary replacement by name.

He ended the call with, "Consider it done."

Chapter Seventeen

Morgan City, Louisiana, USA
4th of February, 10:00 a.m. (GMT-6)

Peter Fontenot was filling up the gas tank and doing the last round of checks before putting the airboat in the water. He usually let it rest for the winter, but his grandmother was a formidable woman. Grand Maman Fontenot, the matriarch of the family, was not a tall or big woman, but she had rule of the roost. When she told him to get the boat ready, he got the boat ready.

When she exited her house, she had three people in tow: a tall, pretty Latina with dark hair and dark eyes in the company of two black men. The older one was on the stout side and the younger was big, like some sort of ebon Thor.

Grand Maman Fontenot came to the water's edge and gave him instructions, "Chère, you're gonna take these folks up to Bayou Chene, wait for them do their business, and bring them back."

"Oui, mémé," he answered obediently and waited for the litany to begin.

She circled the boat with a critical eye. It looked fine, but looks could be deceiving. "Have you checked it for leaks?" she began.

"She's holding air like Tati Lenora," he tried to insert some humor at the expense of his least favorite aunt, but Grand Maman would not be so easily derailed.

"Are the poles and lines good?" she steamed forward.

"Checked them myself as I pulled them out of storage," he verified.

She raised a well-shaped eyebrow. "And the engine?"

"She purrs like a kitten," he attested.

"Are you gassed up?"

"Oui," he answered simply. He knew she was running out of fuel if she was asking the softball questions.

"Even the back-up can?" she persisted.

Peter nodded once. "Like you always tell me to."

She knew he must have forgotten something and ran through her mental list one more time. "What about the rifle in case of gators?" she added after some thought.

"With extra bullets," he replied in the call and response tradition.

She ended the interrogation with a satisfied "bon." He bent down so she could kiss him on both cheeks. "Be careful, mon cher," she affectionately gave him her blessing.

"Oui, mémé," he matched tone for tone.

Then, Grand Maman Fontenot did a 180, literally and figuratively. "Clarence, if there is one hair out of place on this boy's head, you will have to answer to me. Understood?" she fiercely addressed Morris.

Peter watched silently as his five-foot-tall gran grew two feet in mood. He knew that voice and when he was a boy, it was usually followed with a switch. No one gave a whooping like Grand Maman Fontenot. She was both angry and disappointed, although with hindsight, he'd always deserved it. He had heard it been said many a time that he was a naughty and willful child.

Morris gave the petite matriarch a sincere look. "I would walk through fire first," he declared as he brought her hand to his lips. She grinned and fought off a giggle as he planted the gentlest of kisses on it. Peter was not entirely comfortable with what was going on but said nothing. Even in her golden years, Grand Maman Fontenot was her own woman.

She regained her composure and handed a basket to Martinez—food was too important to entrust with men. "For when ya'll get hungry. I packed enough for everyone, and there's bottles of water in there too."

"Thank you, Ms. Fontenot," Martinez replied politely with a slight curtsy. "I'll be sure it gets back to you."

Grand Maman Fontenot liked manners. "Peter, why can't you find a nice girl that respects her elders?"

Peter knew there was no right answer to the question and just let it slide. Instead, he said, "We better get going if we want to get back before dark."

LaSalle helped him position the boat so it was mostly in the water and facing the right way. He stepped on deck and helped Martinez and Morris board before loading their gear.

For someone so tall and swole, he was surprising agile and sure-footed on the flat-bottom boat. Peter sat on top where he could keep watch for obstacles in the water while his passengers took the seats below where the wind would be less rough. The engine roared to life, and the seasoned boatman steered her the rest of the way into the water.

Ms. Fontenot waved them off and watched the airboat shrink from view before heading inside. She told herself that Peter knew the bayou like the back of his hand and Clarence wouldn't let anything happen to him, but a grandmother worries.

Peter didn't open up the engine until they were in open water. Airboats were noisy as hell and didn't provide any cover to those on board, but they could go just about as fast as a same-sized motorboat and would never get stuck on vegetation or the shallows. Peter maintained full throttle, as there was no risk of overheating in this weather and there was nothing about the ensemble that said to take the scenic route.

The airboat was propelled by a column of air generated by a giant fan in back and steering was a matter of directing the airstream with an oversized joystick. For something so simple, it took a skilled hand to operate well. There were no signs, buoys, or flags to guide the way, but Peter knew which bends to follow and which branches to ignore. He'd ferried people to Bayou Chene many times because it was deep in the heart of Atchafalaya Basin. There were no roads going there and if someone wanted to visit, it had to be by boat.

Bayou Chene was first settled by the Cajuns in the 1830s, named after the oak trees that used to litter the place. The Cajuns made the most of the low-lying wetlands others seemed to avoid. They engaged in agriculture, hunting, fishing, cypress logging, and harvesting Spanish moss. Whatever they needed, they either got from the swamp or bought with money earned from its fruits. They built a good life there, and in its heyday, Bayou Chene had homes, schools, churches, grocery stores, and even a post office.

In an effort to minimize the flooding of the Mississippi River in the early twentieth century, the government started diverting water into the Atchafalaya River. By making it a spillway, the isolated wetland was precipitously introduced into a larger network of waterways that deposited large amounts of silt annually. As a result, the careful ecological balance of the Atchafalaya Basin was irreparably changed and the flooding there only got worse.

As traditional Cajun life became more untenable, people left Bayou Chene until there were no more residents at all. Its last living year was 1955, and each flood season brought more sediment. Currently, Bayou Chene was under twelve to eighteen feet of dirt, but it was never forgotten. Each September, its former residents and their descendants took to their boats and made an annual pilgrimage to swap stories, food, and fellowship on top of the remains of their home in the bayou.

The one surviving landmark that hadn't yet yielded to

the Mississippi's silt was a lone gravestone in the Methodist Cemetery. That was where Peter was headed. He slowed the engine as he passed the three-way meet; there were no brakes on airboats and he didn't have a reversible propeller. There were no docks or pull-ups this deep in the bayou and he glided the boat right onto the bank as gentle as rocking a baby to sleep.

As soon as he cut the engine, Morris checked the time. His grandmother wasn't lying—Peter had got them there in no time flat. LaSalle started unloading the gear while Martinez fished out Tupperware containers of food and bottles of water for them and left the rest in the basket on the boat.

Morris drew the young man aside to have a word. "I wanna go over a few things with you while we're gone," he said in low tone with just a little dollop of his will. Peter suddenly felt very honored; he was being taken into confidence instead of just being told what to do.

"First, no matter what you see or hear—or think you see or hear—stay on the boat. If we need you, someone will come back and fetch you. Second, we should be done well before four, but if we are not back by then, I want you to leave. You are not to be here after dark if we have not returned by then."

Peter bobbed his head up and down; there was something a little shady about the situation and he knew better than to ask. "Yes, sir. I understand."

"Say it back to me, so I know you know," Morris coaxed him. He'd made Ms. Fontenot a promise and he intended to keep it.

Peter thought it a strange request but humored the old man. "I will stay on the boat no matter what, and if ya'll don't return by four, I'm to head home without you." As he spoke the words, he knew them to be true—that was exactly what he was going to do.

"Good man. Your grandmother was right—you are sharp." He clapped him on the back and disembarked. "We left you the basket in case you get hungry." Peter watched them walk away, deeper into the city buried under silt.

Much had changed since Morris had last set foot on Bayou Chene. What used to be lakes were now forest and all the oaks were gone, replaced with the sandy-soil-loving willow. Even the water was the wrong color. He set his mental map on where he remembered the Methodist church being and intuited the path.

"This way," he motioned and they headed further inland. Martinez and LaSalle followed, keeping the chatter to a minimum lest they distract him. It didn't take much to draw Morris into conversation. He stopped abruptly and spun in place, giving his brain time to confirm what his feet already knew. "Here," he said definitively. LaSalle pulled out the trenching shovel, while Morris and Martinez unpacked the rest.

The plan itself was straightforward: lure Hugo Dubois out to the bayou and de-poltergeist him. Once he was no longer a malevolent undead being, the going would get a lot easier. They had spent yesterday evening going over contingencies and making preparations. Martinez had picked up the walkie-talkies from the Acadian Village, LaSalle metaphysically deodorized the iron band with baking soda, and Morris made holy water in the bathtub, much to Martinez's surprise.

LaSalle made quick work of the trench, keeping the circle a tight three feet in diameter. The circle was meant to hold the poltergeist—the smaller the area, the less energy it could draw from its surroundings. However, it had to be big enough to chalk the runes and accommodate the three of them standing around it to power the ritual.

Once he was finished, Martinez took over. Even though she was the newest to practicing the arts, Morris said she had the best penmanship of the bunch, although she was pretty sure he was just testing her. The air was still, making it easy for her to chalk the perimeter and runes with a field pen. The refillable chamber was packed with powdered chalk—the kind used at sporting events—and the blunt narrowed tip was ideal for precise deposition of a generous amount of chalk.

She took her time to get it right the first time; the circle wouldn't keep the poltergeist in if she made an error, and there was no easy way to erase a mistake under the circumstances. When she was finished, the white lines and symbols stood out against the dry dark soil. When neither LaSalle nor Morris could find fault with it, they poured salt and holy water into the shallow trench and placed the ring inside the circle as well as a bunch of walkie-talkies with the transmitting buttons taped down. The trap was set; now to bait it.

LaSalle opened his violin case and passed the bow over the block of resin before doing a quick tuning. This was the only speculative part of the plan. Morris liked Martinez's Pied Piper idea, but there was no way to knowing where to go to catch Dubois's ear. Then he remembered the walkie-talkies. If Zoe Miller heard the music in hers through Eva Chapman's, it meant there was a connection—however brief or tentative—between the two devices and the poltergeist. Of course, there had been no way for Martinez to know which walkie-talkies were the ones Chapman and Miller were using that night, so she just took them all. Brute force solutions were still solutions.

The librarians seemed to think it was at least theoretically possible, which was enough for them to proceed. The circle would work regardless how Dubois got there and it was the fussiest part. Once the circle was perfect, there was no harm in trying persuasion over coercion. If the walkie-talkie gambit failed, Morris now knew enough to summon Dubois directly into the circle, but that would regrettably set them on a path of forceful resolution. He wanted to avoid that if possible. Conflict was significantly more draining, but it always made for a solid plan B.

Morris turned to LaSalle. "You ready?" LaSalle cracked his neck and nodded. They each placed a Babel lozenge in their mouth and took their positions around the circle.

LaSalle abutted the end of the violin to his chest just below the collarbone. The old-time music he was going to play wasn't about complicated finger or bow techniques that required a classical stance. It was about keeping the music going and feeling it in your soul. He went inside himself to a place of love and longing where music and magic mingled. He tapped his foot on the ground and the beat pulsed through his body and the bayou. Then he picked up his bow and drew it across the strings along with his summoned will.

He pulled long strokes in the Nova Scotia tradition rather than the more rhythmic, three-finger slide used in Creole style. It was the difference between white and black French music. While they shared many of the same tunes, themes, and traditions, they were definitely played with distinct accents. Hugo Dubois was Acadian from the old country; this was what would call to him.

The notes were haunting and lyrical, dripping with beautiful melancholy. With each long draw, Martinez was sure he was going to run out of bow before he changed directions. He went through the melody once on the violin and changed to chording as he broke into song. There were multiple versions of *Oh Pa Janvier*, but this one was closest to Zoe Miller's description. His sweet, clear tenor soared over the violin chords.

Oh Pa Janvier, donne moi Pauline
Oh no Pauline, Pauline est trop jeune
Oh Pa Janvier c'est la seule que moi je peux aimer
Ouais, c'est la seule que moi je peux aimer dans tout le pays
Oh Pa Janvier donne moi Pauline
Tu vas me faire mourir si tu me la donnes pas

Parce que je l'aime trop, j'aime trop Pauine
Oh Pauline ma chere tite Pauline
Qui moi j'aime autant
Oh Pa Janvier tu me fais trop du mal
Quand tu me refuses, tu me refuses mais Pauline
Oh Pa Janvier tu me creves le coeur
Goodbye. Goodbye. Goodbye pour toujours.

Though he sang in French, Martinez understood each phrase and stanza. *Oh father winter, give me Pauline. She's the only one I can love in the whole country. You're gonna kill me if you don't give her to me because I love her too much. You hurt me too much when you refuse me Pauline. Oh father winter, you break my heart.*

The sky darkened and the wind picked up. Martinez kept an eye on the chalk; the runes and circle were still intact despite the flecks of white fluttering in the air. The walkie-talkies started to crackle with static but the circle was still empty.

When LaSalle finished his verse, he resumed the melody on the strings until the poltergeist was with them. It was a whirling force of rage that was roughly the shape of a man, but its features were distorted, constantly writhing and never knowing stillness.

As soon as it appeared, it tried to leave the circle but found the way blocked. Then it tried to retreat into the land of the dead, but found himself forced to manifest in the mortal realm. It howled in anger, pressing against the unseen forces that caged it in.

Morris held up his large silver cross and rang his ritual bell. The small chime was louder than all the poltergeist's screams, and brought a moment of utter silence to that patch of Bayou Chene. The poltergeist turned to Morris, its face solidifying, and he instantly recognized those eyes.

"Hello, Mr. Dubois," his powerful voice resonated and shook the trees. "I've been looking for you for a while. I'm so glad you could join us."

Chapter Eighteen

Bayou Chene, Louisiana, USA
4th of February, 12:00 p.m. (GMT-6)

Dubois was surprised to be addressed in French; so few here knew the tongue. He was still suspicious of the circle that bound him, but he allowed the attempt to parley. "Why do you call me here with that song?" he asked Morris.

"We've come to return your property to you," Morris answered.

"I have nothing and no one," Dubois solemnly answered. The whirling slowed a little.

Martinez stepped forward and piggybacked her will off Morris's. "Simone sent us here to return your ring, in hopes that it would remind you of happier days and bring you some peace of mind." Dubois scoffed at that—she had cast him aside, not once but twice.

"If you don't believe me, it's on the ground. See for yourself," she pressed lightly.

Dubois spotted the small unassuming iron ring, a symbol for the thing that had sustained him in the depths. He shook his ghostly head. "I do not want it." By now, his legs had taken shape, but his torso was still spinning.

She applied a little more sweetness to her words, a trick she'd picked up from Deacon. "We came all this way. Will you not at least pick it up? It has missed you," she appealed to the gentleman underneath the anger. The spirit's center had set and the swirl of his arms was gradually slowing.

Dubois bent down on his knees and reached for it. He expended the power to touch it, for old time's sake, and his arms settled into form. He was expecting the familiar agony that had accompanied him all those years, but when he made contact, it was no longer there.

For the first time in centuries, he could remember his wedding with fondness. His life was just beginning, with such promise as the girl with dark eyes and yellow ribbons in her hair slipped the ring on his finger. His face softened and he spent a little more energy to put it on, the way she had done once with a heart full of love.

"It feels lighter," the spirit spoke reverently.

Morris met him where he was and extended his will. LaSalle and Martinez bolstered his magic with theirs. "You are not bound to that body anymore. You do not have to be bound to its pain."

Hugo considered his words and saw their merit. The ache was still there, but it no longer burned inside him with the intensity of a thousand suns. As his ethereal body stilled, the iron ring fell to the ground but a ghostly ring remained on his finger. He was no longer a poltergeist. He was now just a ghost with a lot of shit to work through.

It had been so long since he wasn't furious, he didn't know how to carry himself anymore. He stood up straight and pulled his shoulders back, becoming reacquainted with his ghostly form. "Thank you for bringing it to me. I didn't realize how much I had missed it."

"My pleasure, Mr. Dubois," Morris replied.

"Please, call me Hugo," he politely insisted. "I must confess, I'm not sure what I am supposed to do now. I don't belong anywhere."

Morris lay out his options plainly. "If you want to be no more, I can assist you in that. But if you are not quite ready, I know a place you might like. They are not your people, but they hail from them. Maybe you could join their community and start over."

Dubois wanted time to consider the matter, but his energy was dwindling rapidly. It was high noon and he was manifested in front of three people—utterly exhausting for a ghost, even one being fed the magic of three practitioners. "Can I see this place before I decide?"

"Of course, we can show you the way," Morris answered and nodded to his compatriots. LaSalle put his violin and bow back in the case and all three held hands before walking into the circle.

Magic flowed from LaSalle's hands into theirs, and Martinez

felt herself physically disappear even though she retained all her senses. She turned to each side and saw her companions as they were, but she could see through them as she could with herself. She squeezed LaSalle's hand tightly to see if she could feel it, and he squeezed back to let her know they still existed, just in a different form.

The three of them knew where they were going, but for Dubois's benefit, LaSalle simply said, "Follow me, it's right this way." With Martinez in one hand and Morris in the other, LaSalle stepped into the earth. As soon as Dubois entered the silt, the fatigue lifted and he felt revitalized. Martinez, however, felt unbearably cold, which didn't make sense because she didn't currently have a body. With one ghostly foot in the ground, she pushed aside such thoughts and continued walking, repeating in her mind what LaSalle had told her earlier. *Everything is going to be fine as long as I don't let go.*

After a few steps, they were back in the bayou, only this one was full of oak and cypress draped with Spanish moss. It was night and the ground was covered in mist. A light cut through the fog and LaSalle walked toward it. More lights popped into view as they neared a house lit by lanterns, beacons for the lost to find their way back.

The door was wide open, and the sound of music and dancing spilled onto the front lawn where a fire that gave no heat crackled. The large pot hanging over it bubbled nonetheless, and it was constantly stirred by a man having a smoke. When he saw them emerge from the mist, he waved them down. As they neared, he squinted and pulled his pipe out of his mouth. "Clarence?! Is that you?" he called out. "Don't tell me he finally got you and sent you here."

"Jacques!" Morris waved back with his free hand while the other firmly clamped to LaSalle's. "I'm just passing through, but I brought someone who might stay a while, if you'll have him."

"The more the merrier!" the ghostly cook declared. "How are you called?" he addressed Dubois.

"Hugo," he answered without giving a last name.

"A man without a surname. I like him already," Jacques said to Morris. "And what's your story, Hugo?" Dubois hesitated, uncertain what to say.

"He died in Le Grand Dérangement and just found out his wife remarried after his death," Morris helped ease the introductions.

"Ah, *la femme*," Jacques sighed wistfully. "Bet she married a real louse, too."

"My cousin," Dubois replied with derision.

"Well, there are plenty of bewitching beauties with broken hearts that need mending, too. Good-looking feller like you should have no problems. It's ugly old cusses like Clarence and me that gotta develop charisma," Jacques jested. LaSalle couldn't hold back a smile.

Dubois sniffed at the pot. "You hungry?" Jacques asked. "I

just started this mess of mudbugs, but there's some ready inside with corn on the cob and boiled potatoes. Go on and get you some hot food and a cold drink before the next song starts." Dubois froze. He didn't know what to do with the invitation. It felt good to be welcomed, but he wasn't sure if he wanted to go in.

"Excuse us, Jacques, we have some deliberating to do," Morris said as he made a tactical retreat on Dubois's behalf.

Jacques put his pipe back in his mouth and puffed away. "You go deliberate," he shooed them while he stirring the pot. "You know where to find me." Martinez was struck at how substantial the man felt compared to the smoke, even though they were both transparent. Only the smoke seemed ephemeral.

They all moved away from the house but kept the lights in sight. "What do you think?" Morris asked Dubois when they were out of earshot. "Do you want to stay? Or would you like me to help you dissipate?" He knew Dubois's answer before he even asked—Deacon had been at this a long time—but gave the man time to come to it himself.

As in life, Dubois kept his own council and looked back at the house, full of life and music. It was a little daunting, but also exciting. It had been a long time since he'd had that feeling. "If it's all the same to you, I think I'd like to stay. I spent a long time in oblivion. I think I'd like to live a little more before I meet my maker."

Morris shook Dubois's hand with his free one. "*Bon chance,*

Hugo."

"*Merci,*" the ghost bid them before returning to the house and closing the door. As it closed, Martinez saw a small smile beneath the formerly ferocious eyes.

The trio walked out of the earth and back into the light. The weak sun warmed Martinez's soul; she promised to never complain about winter again, not even Detroit's. As LaSalle ended his spell, she could feel his magic eek out of her body. She was once again flesh and bones, but she held onto his hand a little longer to make sure it was real.

Morris left the pair and took the shovel in hand. He dug a foot straight down and dropped the iron ring into the hole. LaSalle took the shovel from him and made quick work of returning the soil to where it had just been. Then he turned the chalked soil over into the trench before backfilling the area and leveling it off. Any sign of disturbance would be gone with the next flood.

They packed the rest of their gear in silent reflection. Visiting the land of the dead had a way of doing that. It made everything gray, thin, and hollow. When they were ready to leave, Morris took a knee and patted the mound. "Au revoir, Mr. Dubois. *Lâche pas la patate.*"

Chapter Nineteen

Lafayette, Louisiana, USA
4th of February, 9:30 p.m. (GMT-6)

"I told you, it's all about energy," Morris said emphatically over the din of the bar. It was three dollar pitcher night and the band was playing zydeco. "Reduce the input, increase expenditure, and the storm can no longer sustain itself." He tipped his cup back.

"Clarence, you're drunk," Martinez called him out.

"No," he protested. "Tipsy at best."

"Clarence doesn't need to be drunk to turn braggadocious," LaSalle snidely remarked before taking a swig.

"Look who got a word a day calendar for Christmas," Morris verbally parried. "And it's not bragging if it's true."

Martinez interrupted their bickering and held up her index finger. "I have one question." Which wasn't true at all. It had been a strange few days and she had a lot of questions, but she knew she didn't have enough time or beer to process all of that tonight. Instead, she'd settle for the one sticking point that nagged at her. "How did you know the ring wasn't going to backfire and just make him more pissed?" she asked.

"First, because you presented it to him, and everything sounds nicer coming from a sweet young thing—"

"Dangerously close to inappropriate, Deacon," she cautioned him.

He tactically rephrased and tried again, "What I'm trying to say is that in Mr. Dubois's time, there are certain things men would be more receptive to talking about with women than other men, and feelings is one of them." Martinez waved her hand to signal that was acceptable and he could proceed pontificating.

"And two, anyone that upset by losing a woman is a romantic underneath it all. He still cared and by showing up with that ring, it let him know that some part of her still cared too," he explained.

"And you don't think we let him off too lightly?" she inquired. "He did kill eleven people and we basically dropped him off at a kitchen party."

His jovial mood turned very serious. "We're not here to punish or pass judgment. We're here to contain and neutralize. Causing him further pain and torment was not going to bring those people back, and I gave those souls what peace I could."

She thought it over with a long drink. "I hear what you're saying, but it still feels wrong in my gut."

"That's the Catholic in you. Guilt and punishment are two sides of the same coin," he stated as fact.

That made Martinez look away and smile. She turned to

LaSalle. "I'm going for another pitcher. I want to see what pearls of wisdom come out of him if we ply him with more beer." As she waded into the crowd and nudged her way to the bar, the band came back from break with drinks in hand and started another set.

"Did you know most of the Cajun songs are in three-quarters time because they were meant to be danced to?" Morris laid thick the innuendo on that factoid.

LaSalle shook his head. "Old man, say what you gonna say." His crisp annunciation faded away, in part because of the beer but also because it was just him and Deacon.

Morris leaned in so he could be heard. "If you don't ask that girl to dance, I will."

"I don't think she'd appreciate you calling her a girl," LaSalle pointed out.

"Boy, don't talk semantics with me!" Morris said indignantly. "You know just as well as I do she's a tough nut. She barely shed two tears when I put five to rest. Hobgoblin cried like a baby for thirty minutes the first time he saw me do one, and he's no wimp."

Morris wasn't telling LaSalle anything he didn't already know. The first time he put her through the process—the magical ritual he performed to ensure Salt Mine agents were not compromised in the field—it took so much out of him, he needed water, food, and a nap. But he kept his poker face up and took another gulp of beer. "What's your point, Clarence?"

"My point is, you're not gonna break her on accident, so all you have to do is make sure you don't do it on purpose." He didn't use his will, but the stated and unsaid truths struck LaSalle just as deep.

LaSalle finished his drink and retreated into stoicism. "I don't do that anymore."

"I know that," Morris said with exasperation. "That's why I'm telling you to ask her to dance."

LaSalle traced the rim of his empty glass with his thumb. "I like her, but I don't want to lead her on and make her think there's a future here."

"That's fair," Morris readily agreed. "I mean, smart, strong, determined women who build a career at the FBI are known to drop everything for a diamond ring and white wedding. And everyone knows signing up at the Mine is really just the fast track to baby town."

The minute changes to LaSalle's face told him the message was received, so he dialed down the sarcasm and got real with his junior. "David, don't overthink it. Sometimes a dance is just a dance."

LaSalle let out a short laugh. "That sounds like something Teresa would say."

Morris nodded with approval. "See, she's wise, too. You're lucky I'm not a younger man."

"Clarence, you were born old," LaSalle retorted.

Martinez emerged out of crowd with a pitcher in each hand.

"Figured it would save us a trip later," she justified doubling down. She refilled everyone's glass and took a seat. "What did I miss? I want to hear all the truth bombs and burns."

"I was just enumerating the ways David is a dumbass," Morris said before taking a swallow off the top.

"Now Clarence, that's not nice. He put his vacation on pause to help you. And don't pretend you weren't just saying how you missed him at work yesterday morning," she chastised him in the style of Grand Maman Fontenot.

LaSalle grinned at that. "Aw, did you miss me, Clarence?" he taunted in a precious voice.

Martinez slapped her hand on LaSalle's ridiculously large bicep. "Don't you start! I'm trying to get him to apologize to you."

LaSalle and Morris exchanged looks and burst out laughing. Martinez was genuinely confused. "What's so funny?"

LaSalle wiped a tear from his eye. "Morris, in all the time we've known each other, have you ever apologized to me for anything?" he asked the older black man.

"Can't say I recall ever doing any wrong by you," he replied on cue.

"I rest my case," LaSalle said as he raised his glass and tipped it back.

Martinez gave up on making them play nice. "You two fight like an old married couple."

LaSalle put his glass down with conviction. "Would you

like to dance?" he asked Martinez before he had time to think about it. The question took her by surprise and a few seconds passed before she realized it was directed at her.

"And leave him with all the beer?" She tried to play coy but it was too late. Her eyes had already said yes.

"Think of what will come out of his mouth after he drinks all that," LaSalle went along with the ruse. He stood up and offered his hand. "What do you say?"

She didn't know what possessed LaSalle to behave so against type, but she wasn't going to question it. Not after the day she'd had. "Why not? We're in Cajun country—*laissez les bons temps rouler*." Her pronunciation was atrocious, but LaSalle didn't care. She'd said yes.

"Clarence, watch the beer," she ordered him before taking one last sip and putting her hand in LaSalle's. He led her out to the floor and put his right hand in the middle of her back. She closed the posture by rested her left hand on his arm. The band was hot and playing fast, and it felt a little like trying to enter the freeway from a dead stop. Undeterred, LaSalle guided her with a steady hand and found a gap.

They whirled with the mass of dancers, most in various states of inebriation. He steered through the chaos until he found a spot he liked the look of. Before Martinez knew what was happening, he released his hand on her back and she spun with just the lead of his long fingertips. Before she knew it, she did something she wasn't proud of—she wooed in delight.

She wasn't a "woo girl" by nature, but she hadn't danced with someone who really knew how to lead before. Just as she finished her spin, she was back in his arms and on the move.

When the music slowed, he matched its meter. There was no lightning fiddle or accordion solos, just a sweet melody for them to sway in closed position. The band played soft enough to allow conversation and Martinez couldn't resist goading him a little.

"I'm learning all sorts of things about you today," she said impishly. "You play the violin. You have a beautiful singing voice. You speak French." She slowly listed them, deliberately leaving out all the supernatural stuff. "And now, I know you can dance."

"Deacon isn't the only one with *joie de vivre*," he slyly replied.

"Can I ask you something?" she murmured over the music. She felt his body tense but it was hard to tell if it was from her question or just the dancing.

"Sure," he replied.

"Why did the Salt Mine recruit me?"

It caught him off guard but he recovered quickly. It wasn't the type of question he was expecting and he didn't know what kind of answer she was looking for. He decided to play it safe. "You were a good candidate with a career that adequately prepared you for the job. And after the incident," he alluded to one of her last cases before joining the Salt Mine, "Leader knew you had the right temperament."

She brushed off his generic explanation. "I figured all that out. I mean *why?*" She emphasized the last word. "Everyone's got something that they do really well. But I'm a year in, and I don't feel like I've found my *special* skill."

"Why ask me?" he wondered. Chloe and Dot had trained her from day one and they had a good relationship, last he'd heard.

"At the Mine, you probably know the most about me: background checks, all my reports, the process. Everyone I work with sees a piece, but you've seen them all," she reasoned.

LaSalle was a witness and keeper of many things, but he'd never thought about how it must seem the other way around. How intrusive it was. And unbalanced. He knew all these things about her and she so little about him, yet she'd followed him into the land of the dead and trusted that he would lead her back. When was the last time he'd been asked to take such a leap of faith, and when was the last time he'd actually taken it?

He leaned in. There was so much he couldn't tell her, but at least he could tell her more about herself. "I don't know if this is your special skill, but I do know you are obstinately *you* to your core."

She pulled back. "Are you calling me stubborn?" she said defensively.

"No," he quickly rejected the notion in the strongest terms

and breathed a little easier once she relaxed back into his arms. He chose his words better before opening his mouth again. "You're hard to affect, special-wise," he used her code.

"But I have no problem practicing and playing well with others," she said euphemistically.

"Because you wanted to do. Think back—have you ever been forced or coerced into doing something you didn't want to do? I'd bet even the things you came to later regret, you wanted to do in the moment," he wagered a guess.

Martinez looked unconvinced, and LaSalle trawled his memory for examples. "Remember your first time across the pond?" he alluded to the reacquisition of the Midas Coin. "Anyone else would be have been knocked out, but you were able to regain your footing and take the shot. Or the time Alicia got in trouble in Greece?" He didn't have to say Magh Meall or waters of Narcissus to jog her memory. "You were able to get her out. She's no novice, but *you* were the one that kept your wits about you. And the stuffed dinosaur." The way he said it, it wasn't a question, but a statement of fact. Martinez shuttered at the thought of Furfur trying to charm her. "I was there when you returned with it. You were still you."

"It wasn't like they didn't impact me," she objected. "You don't know how badly I wanted to roll down the meadow."

"But you didn't," he reiterated his point. "You're not invulnerable or immune, but it's a lot harder for things to target you because that involves bending you to their will. And you don't bend unless you want to. At least, not easily. In this job, that's a good thing."

Martinez bit her lip while she digested all this. She had asked for truth bombs but she'd expected them to be dropped by Morris in an entertaining fashion, like fireworks for the soul. This felt more like a depth charge. She let him glide her across the floor while she considered his theory, comforted by the movement and contact.

"Damned if my mother wasn't right. I am the most stubborn person on the planet," she begrudgingly gave credit where it was due.

"Do you want to go back to the table," he offered.

"No, I'm good," she answered immediately. When the thought crossed her mind that this could be his way of saying he wanted to stop dancing, she looked up and added, "But we can if you want to."

He looked into her brown eyes, the color of a stirred cappuccino and still a little soft and fuzzy from the beer even with all the serious talk of late. "No, I'm good, too," he replied with a smile.

She smiled back. "Then let's just keep dancing."

She put her head on his chest where he'd braced his violin and played the saddest song she'd ever heard. He slid his hand around her back and pulled her in a little closer.

Morris watched them from the side, pleased with himself. A man needs a community and a purpose. And if he is so blessed, someone to share that with. That was Hugo's problem—he was alone for too long and left with only his thoughts. That was a bad combination for many a man.

He was refilling his glass when a sultry voice spoke up behind him. "You look like you could use some company." She had long silky hair, large brown eyes, a pretty smile, and what he referred to as that big leg, tight skirt look. "Mind if I join you?" she asked suggestively.

"Nice try, but I know it's you," he said flatly and took a sip of beer.

Her voice changed from milk and honey to sour grapes. "What gave me away? She's exactly your type."

"Women that look like that don't go around picking up guys that look like me," he explained.

"She could have been fishing for you to buy her a drink?" the bitter voice came out of the luscious full-lipped mouth.

"With the cheap stuff I have on the table? She'd have to be touched to pick me for that," he replied.

"But if she's not attractive enough, you won't be interested at all." It raged so vigorous it swayed her ample bosom.

Morris nodded in agreement, staring intensely at the womanly form before him. "You've just stumbled on the great paradox of desire. No one wants what they can get, and no one gets what they want."

The voice turned ugly and growled, "I caught you in the crossroads once, Clarence. I'll catch you again."

Beer in hand, Morris replied, "Maybe you will, maybe you will. But not tonight, Satan."

Epilogue

The authorities had not yet released the remains found at the Acadian Village, but the family saw no reason to drag it out any longer. There was no doubt that Eva Chapman was dead and it was time to mourn her. Without remains, there was no reason to engage a funeral home and they held a memorial at her church instead.

They waited until the weekend, to give plenty of notice and make it easier for everyone to attend. The local paper listed the service's time and location at the end of the obituary, right after the list of who had passed before her and who had survived her. Her kids came back to make the arrangements and found their childhood home much the same as they had left it, only emptier without their mom there.

Eva would have been pleased by the turnout. It felt like the whole city was jammed inside the Good News Baptist Church. Everyone came to pay their respects and the pews were packed. Even her ex-husband came, though he knew better than to take a seat in the front two rows reserved for family. Those were for her children and grandchildren, who played their part solemnly, and her siblings and their families. If there was one blessing in all this, it was that her parents were not alive to see what happened to their little girl.

There was talk about the gruesome details—that couldn't be helped—but everyone left that at the door when they entered the house of God. The front was covered with flowers as well as an enlarged photo of Eva placed on an easel—the same picture that was in the paper. The church had brought in a professional photographer for family portraits a few years ago, and Eva put on her best hat and came as a family of one. There was music and the choir sang her favorite hymns. The preacher gave a lovely eulogy and a stirring message of hope—despair not, Eva was now with God. There were a lot of amens and open weeping. It was everything church should be.

While the memorial was open to the public, the home visitation afterward was limited to close friends and family. A light lunch was of course provided, but everyone brought a dish or plate of something with them. Food was love and Eva was beloved. It was up to all of them to make sure her family felt loved now that she was gone. The end result was enough food to feed ten times the number of people. There was the typical cries of "Where are we going to put all this food?" but they weren't really complaints. They were part of the chorus of mourning.

Zoe Miller parked her silver Corolla along the street two

blocks down from Eva's house. She wasn't officially invited, but neither were half the people in attendance. Everyone wanted to give their condolences personally and thought they counted as close friends. The rush allowed Zoe to enter under the radar and do a lap to get her bearings.

The house was full of adults and small children shuffling around with food and drink while the older kids were outside playing in their good clothes, a pack that was collectively called "the cousins." Not all of them were blood, but they were family.

The furniture had been rearranged to accommodate visitors, but no one had anticipated quite this many close friends and family. They ran out of seats well before they would run out of food, and those that were seated readily relinquished their seats to older folks and ladies in a long game of musical chairs.

Zoe had never met Eva's kids before, but she'd seen plenty of pictures and saw them at the service. The eldest was Michael and the younger one Esther. Both them were older than her, but Esther by only a few years. She was in the kitchen trying to sooth a fussy baby on one hip while Michael played man of the house in the living room, mostly to stop his father from trying to.

Zoe grabbed a plate of food and bid her time in a quiet corner, waiting for her moment. She watched the flow of in and out until she spotted her moment—brother and sister alone with no kids, spouses, or well-wishers. She avoided the living room, filled with people reminiscing and telling stories, and aimed for the back door via the kitchen. She heard raised voices as soon as she got to the fridge, bickering the way siblings do even after they become adults with kids of their own. Old habits die hard.

"So it's my fault Mom's dead?" Esther asked, incensed. "Excuse me for wanting to have a life of my own."

"I'm not saying it's anyone's fault, but someone should have been here watching out for her," Michael reiterated his point.

"She wasn't some elderly shut-in with poor health or a failing mind, Michael. She was an independent woman in her fifties with a good job and tons of friends," she argued, waving her hand toward the packed house.

"Friends aren't the same as family," he said seriously.

"It's easy to tell me I should have stayed, but you could have moved back at any time," she reminded him.

"You know Allison couldn't leave her parents," he objected.

"And Allison's parents are more important than Mom was? Now who's the Judas?" she struck back.

Zoe made some noise in the kitchen and the argument abruptly stopped. She counted to ten before exiting. "Hi. I didn't mean to disturb you. I just wanted to tell you how sorry am I about your mother's passing."

It was a variation of a sentiment that had been repeated all day. "Thank you. That's very kind of you to say," Esther automatically said for the millionth time.

"You should know that either of you being here wouldn't

have stopped this from happening," Zoe tried to comfort them.

The siblings exchanged looks and were suddenly a united front. "I'm sorry, who are you again?" Michael pointedly asked.

"I know you don't know me," Zoe qualified, "but I worked with your mom and we came to be friends. I was working the day she disappeared and when the police found her remains," she answered them without giving her name.

The mention of the macabre circumstances silenced them and Michael had to take a seat. "The police said all that was left were her bones. What kind of sick person does that?"

"I saw him. He just looked like a normal guy," Zoe replied.

"That's what people always say about serial killers," Esther said conspiratorially.

Zoe had practiced many variations of the same speech, and this wasn't going at all how she'd planned. But a promise is a promise. "I don't know if I'm out of turn for saying this, but your mom recently told me she was really proud of both of you for getting out. She loved you too much to hold you back, even if it meant she didn't see her grandchildren as much."

Michael looked up. "Did she really say that?" he asked.

"Yeah," Zoe added a nod so there was no mistaking her answer. "She'd bake up a storm and bring it by the office so she wouldn't eat it all. We'd sit and have coffee, and she'd sneak a few in anyway," she recalled fondly.

Esther smiled and rubbed her brother's back like their mother used to do when he was upset as a kid. "That does sound like Mom."

Michael coughed back some tears. "She did love her grandbabies."

"Sometimes too much—spoiled them rotten! She never bought us all those fancy toys at Christmas when we were kids," Esther complained, but her tone and face weren't angry.

Her older brother chuckled. "No doubt, but there were always plenty of Santa-shaped cookies."

"She did make the best cut-out cookies," Esther agreed with her brother.

Zoe awkwardly shuffled her feet. "Well, that's all I wanted to say. I know you have a house full of visitors. I won't take up any more of your time."

Esther put her hand on Zoe's arm and paused her retreat. "Thank you for stopping by."

THE END

The agents of The Salt Mine will return in *Vicious Circle*

Printed in Great Britain
by Amazon